STATION JIM

Also by Louis de Bernières

FICTION
Labels and Other Stories
So Much Life Left Over
Blue Dog
The Dust that Falls from Dreams
Notwithstanding: Stories from an English Village
A Partisan's Daughter
Birds Without Wings
Red Dog
Sunday Morning at the Centre of the World
Captain Corelli's Mandolin
The Troublesome Offspring of Cardinal Guzman
Señor Vivo and the Coca Lord
The War of Don Emmanuel's Nether Parts

NON-FICTION
The Book of Job: An Introduction

POETRY
The Cat in the Treble Clef
Of Love and Desire
Imagining Alexandria
A Walberswick Goodnight Story

STATION JIM

LOUIS DE BERNIÈRES

ILLUSTRATED BY EMMA CHICHESTER CLARK

Harvill *Secker*

LONDON

1 3 5 7 9 10 8 6 4 2

Harvill Secker, an imprint of Vintage,
20 Vauxhall Bridge Road,
London SW1V 2SA

Harvill Secker is part of the Penguin Random House
group of companies whose addresses can be found at
global.penguinrandomhouse.com

Penguin
Random House
UK

First published by Harvill Secker in 2019

A CIP catalogue record for this book is available from the British Library

penguin.co.uk/vintage

ISBN 9781787301610

Typeset in 13/18.5 pts Bembo
by Integra Software Services Pvt. Ltd, Pondicherry

Printed and bound in Italy by L.E.G.O. S.p.A.

itted to a sustainable future for our
lanet. This book is made from
uncil® certified paper.

STATION JIM

One evening in early spring, in the days when all the trains were driven by steam, an assistant stationmaster found something abandoned on a train. It was at the end of a long day's work, and he was very tired and grumpy, because the public is sometimes most obstreperous and hard to deal with, and he had been on his feet a great deal.

Back then the carriages were divided up into separate compartments, without any connecting corridor. This was a good thing if you got one to yourself, and a bad thing if you had to share it with people who were pestiferous, smelly, smoky, nosy, over-talkative, or so fat that you got squashed. If you had one to yourself you always dreaded it when you reached a station, in case someone horrible decided to come into your carriage. Perhaps the worst thing was that if you were dying for the loo, you had to wait until the next station, and then nip into the public ones, hoping that the train had not gone before you came back out.

The compartments were homely, with a netting parcel rack above the seats, and small posters advertising holiday destinations, such as Great Yarmouth or Lyme Regis. The woodwork was heavily varnished, and the seats were extremely bouncy, so that fathers and mothers were always having to tell their children to sit still and behave. You could open the windows, and lean out, even though there were notices telling you not to, and if you did, you sometimes got a wet smut in your eye. If you felt sick and stuck your head out of the window to do it, your sick would fly out of yours and go straight back into the next window along. You could also open the doors when the train was moving, so that you often saw people jumping out at the platform before it had actually stopped, or running for a door when it had already begun to depart. It was altogether more fun when trains were like this, but more dangerous too. You sometimes even saw children collecting conkers from the railway line. Perhaps the most fun thing was that more often than not there were no lights, so that when you went into a tunnel everything suddenly went pitch-black. This gave the children an opportunity to scream with pretend terror, and for people in love to sneak a kiss.

People remember that in those days the summers were very long and hot, which may be because they really were, or because they used to wear an awful lot of clothes. They often had so much luggage that every station had porters to help them carry it, and many people sent their luggage in advance, in large trunks, which would be collected from their houses and delivered to their destinations. Eventually your trunk would get plastered with stickers, and an old person looking at theirs would have a perfect record of everywhere they had ever been. Mine was blue, and bound together with wooden hoops, and it has been in my father's attic for forty years, but once upon a time I could put into it practically everything I owned.

The steam trains on the Great Western Railway were handsome, and gleamed with polished brass and beautiful paintwork. The locomotives had marvellous names, such as *La France, The Great Bear, The City of Truro, The Albion,* and many of the railway workers were extremely proud of them. They certainly did take a lot of caring for, possibly even more than a horse. They took hours to warm up in the morning, and needed enormous amounts of coal that were shovelled into the fire compartment by a stoker who was invariably rippling with muscles, and covered in coal dust from head to foot. The moving parts would need oiling and greasing and inspecting, and there was a big tank of water at every station so that the engines could be replenished through a big floppy canvas tube. This is why you often had time to nip out to the loo.

Mr Leghorn was a proper dyed-in-the-wool railway-man, like his father before him. He loved his steam trains, had worked for only one railway company, the GWR, and expected to work for it for the rest of his days. His brothers worked for the same company, and his sisters worked in a huge house outside Bristol whose owners were hardly ever there. It had to be kept in a state of readiness, even so.

Mr Leghorn had a big moustache, and a head that was mostly bald. His nickname was 'Ginger' because that had been his colour before his hair went white and fell out. This nickname was often shortened to 'Ginge'. He was neither tall nor short, and neither fat nor thin. He had kindly blue eyes, and his complexion was somewhat florid, possibly because he liked to drink a lot of beer during his time off, and he smoked a pipe because in those days no one had any idea that it was bad for you. He smelled of beer and tobacco, which is pretty horrid, so it was lucky for him that so many others smelled exactly the same. He wore a smart uniform, which was not, however, as smart as the uniform he wore when he was out parading with the yeomanry.

At the end of his working day Mr Ginger Leghorn had to check in the carriages and compartments for lost property and for passengers who had accidentally fallen asleep, and ended up in a siding at the wrong station. There used to be a song that went 'Oh! Mister Porter, what shall I do? I want to go to Birmingham, and they're taking me on to Crewe.'

On the day that concerns us, he found something rather unusual, all on its own in a compartment about halfway along the train. He took his cap off, scratched his head, and said 'Blimey, what's this then?' even though he knew perfectly well what it was.

He was quite used to finding things that had been left behind. Today he had already found two umbrellas, one a lady's and the other a gentleman's. It was nearly always umbrellas that he found, but in his time he had found fishing rods, accordions, folding card tables and silver teapots. He had once even found someone who was dead, but this was the first time he had ever found a tiny puppy.

OH GAWD, WHAT AM I GOING TO DO WITH THIS?

Mr Leghorn took off his cap and scratched his head. 'Oh Gawd,' he said to himself, 'what am I going to do with this?'

Mr Leghorn was not, in general, an animal lover, but he did have a shed full of racing pigeons of which he was very fond. They all had fanciful names and pedigrees, and they were extremely smart. Because Mr Leghorn could go wherever he wanted on the railway for free, he sometimes liked to take a couple of pigeons a long way away, and release them from a basket. His long-suffering wife, Mrs Leghorn, was under strict instructions to make a note of the exact time when the pigeons returned, but she was always busy, and not particularly interested, and so she made the times up. Poor Mr Leghorn believed he had record-breaking pigeons, when in reality they were a bunch of saunterers, grain-gatherers and socialisers. He never could understand why it was that he had won no races, and would lie awake at night bothering about it.

Mrs Leghorn's first name was Mary, but everybody called her Molly. She was a cat lover, and she had a big fluffy tabby cat, originally called Matilda. Because someone had not been very good at sexing kittens, it had eventually transpired that Matilda was in fact a boy. In one respect this was a relief, because then Mrs Leghorn did not have to worry about what to do with all the kittens, but in another sense it was an embarrassment to have a tom cat with a girl's name. Then someone who had learned Latin at school told her that all you had to do was change the 'a' into an 'us' or an 'o' and you would have a sort of boy's name. In this way Matilda became Matildo, and he never noticed the difference. Quite often he was addressed as Tildo, and most people assumed it was a pet name for Tiddles, which, in those days, was a very common name for cats. Mostly he was just called Puss.

It will already have occurred to all sensible and knowledgeable readers that it must be a serious mistake to keep a cat and a flock of pigeons in the same place. Tildo, however, was like most cats, in that he was not at all interested in chasing or catching things that made no effort to get away. He would sit in the yard with the pigeons pecking at corn all around him, his mind far away in imaginary mountains and jungles, thinking about all the wild creatures that he would like to pounce on. This was a great relief to both Mr and Mrs Leghorn, because the one could not have done without his pigeons, and the other could not have done without her cat.

It will also have occurred to all sensible and knowledgeable readers that a full-grown cat is likely to be very put out by the arrival of a tiny puppy. When Mr Leghorn came home with one in his arms, and put it down on the kitchen floor, Tildo's tail puffed up like a bottle brush. He arched his back, hissed, marched up to the unfortunate little dog, and scratched it across the nose. The dog yelped and whined, and Tildo stalked back to his chair and glared down frighteningly, his big round eyes full of hatred and disgust.

'Oh Gawd,' said Mr Leghorn, who was already in quite enough of a lather.

Mrs Leghorn was squeezing her washing through the mangle in the backyard, and was in quite a sweat from heaving on the handle, but she came in when she heard the puppy yelp. 'Blimey, love, what's this?' she said rhetorically.

'Abandoned. Found it in a compartment. Thought I'd better bring it home. I didn't know what else to do. I couldn't exactly put it in the locker with all the umbrellas.'

'Someone's bound to claim it,' said Mrs Leghorn.

'I hope so. I don't want it. I've got enough to worry about, what with the pigeons an' all. S'pose we can feed it on scraps.'

'The scraps are Tildo's,' said Mrs Leghorn.

'Well, he's going to have to share. For the time being anyway.'

'How could anyone leave a puppy by accident?' said Mrs Leghorn. 'It don't seem very probable to me.'

'Nor me neither,' said her husband.

'I hope we don't get stuck with it.'

'We can give it away. Someone's bound to want a dog. Lots of people'd like a dog.'

'Well, the kids would,' said Mrs Leghorn.

'Oh Gawd, don't say that.'

But she had said it, and when the children dribbled home one by one, they definitely had an opinion.

The Leghorns had five children, Alfie, Arthur, Beryl, Sissy and Albert, in that order. Although they were equally scruffy and grimy, they were in neatly ascending size, and looked rather alike, so that they appeared to be a complete set of English Russian dolls. In term time they were packed off every morning with their satchels and sandwiches, their clothes clean and their faces scrubbed, but in the holidays Mrs Leghorn often had no idea where they were. There were no cars to mow anyone down, and the neighbourhood's children mostly played in the street, kicking and throwing balls, breaking windows by accident, and engaged in wonderful games that nobody knows how to play any more, such as British Bulldog and Grandmother's Footsteps. When the children were not in the street they were up on the hillside above the railway cottages, poking into rabbit holes with sticks, or rolling down on their sides. When it snowed, they stole the tin trays from their houses, and hurtled down the slopes on them, even though the only way of stopping was to crash into a fence.

The days were long and warm now, and the children could have been anywhere, being fed butter and strawberry jam sandwiches in whichever house they happened to be. They all knew, however, that at half past five on most days Dad came home for his tea, and they would be having tea too. Inside their stomachs they had infallible timing devices that informed them when it was time to go home and eat supper, and then, later on at bedtime, they would get a cup of cocoa and a slice of bread with dripping.

At half past five the Leghorn children came home, bleeding, bruised, tired and contented, and saw the puppy, which was under the table, hiding from Tildo.

ENYWON WANT A PUPY?

Alfie, Arthur, Beryl, Sissy and Albert went down on their hands and knees and peered beneath the folds of the tablecloth.

'Ooh, it's sweet!' said Beryl.

'Is it an Alsatian?' asked Alfie, who wanted an Alsatian because in those days they were bred to be fierce, and were used as guard and police dogs.

'I dunno,' said Mr Leghorn. 'It's hard to tell. I don't know how to tell what a little dog's going to grow into.'

'It is black and brown,' said Arthur.

'It'll probably grow up black and brown, then,' said Mr Leghorn.

'Will it be big?' asked Sissy.

'I don't know how to tell that either.'

'Is it a boy or a girl?' asked Beryl.

'That I do know. It's a boy dog.'

'Oh good,' said Arthur, and Sissy punched him on the arm with one knuckle extended from her fist, which was how the other girls at school had taught her to deal with boys. She hardly ever scratched or bit, however, although she had been known to pinch.

'I want a big dog,' said Albert.

'It's not ours,' said Mr Leghorn. 'Somebody might ring lost property, and claim it back, so it's no use wanting any size of dog at present. We'll have to wait and see.'

Nobody rang lost property, not even after a week, so Mr Leghorn tried one last, desperate thing to get rid of the puppy. It wasn't that he did not like it, in fact he was already very fond of it; it was simply that he felt he had enough to deal with in his life, what with difficult customers, late trains, five children, a cat, and a loft full of racing pigeons that never won any races.

Beryl and Sissy caught him out, though. They were passing the post office when they noticed a postcard in the window. Now, Mr Leghorn's writing was very distinctive. He wrote in large letters, his writing was not joined up, and he had perfectly dreadful spelling, which was not because he was stupid, but because he had had to leave school at ten, in order to go to work when his father died.

The sign that Beryl and Sissy saw was

Enywon want a pupy? Noy suer how old. Very sweet and wel behayvd. Prity much houstraned already. Afrade of cats. Blak and tan. Aply Number 4 Railway Cottiges.

'Number 4 Railway Cottages is us,' said Beryl.

'Sneaky old Dad,' said Sissy.

'There's only one thing to do,' said Beryl.

'Is there?'

'Yes, come on!' Beryl tugged her sister into the post office and approached the wicket.

'Good morning, Miss Beryl,' said the man behind the wicket. 'What can I do for you? Been sent out for stamps?'

'No, Mr Cramp,' replied Beryl. 'It's about that dog notice my dad put up.'

'Oh yes? What about it then?'

'Dad sent me to tell you he wants it to be taken down.'

'Decided to keep it then?'

'Yes, Mr Cramp.'

Mr Cramp smiled and nodded his head wisely. 'That's what nearly always happens. Same with kittens.'

He came out from behind his counter and went to the window to remove Mr Leghorn's card, presenting it to

Beryl, who took it from his hand with a 'Thank you, Mr Cramp'.

'Are you children going to be helping with the harvest this year?' asked Mr Cramp.

'I 'speck so,' said Sissy.

'Well,' said Mr Cramp, 'that's what these long holidays are for, after all. Can't spend all your time just gallivanting.'

'No,' replied Beryl.

After they had gone some few paces down the cobbled street, Sissy said, 'What are we going to do with that card?'

Beryl thought, and said, 'P'raps we should burn it.'

'What with? You got any matches?'

'Course not.'

'We could hide it.'

'What if it gets found?'

When they reached home the children had a parliament in the pigeon loft about what to do with the card, and voted for Alfie's plan, which was to fold it up into a small boat, and drop it off the bridge and let it float away down the river.

Accordingly, Alfie folded the card up, pressing the creases very tightly, so that one way up it looked like a hat, and the other way up it looked like a ship. They slipped out of the back gate, and trooped down to the river.

They argued about who was going to drop it into the water, but of course Alfie won because he had made the boat, and he was the biggest and oldest. 'It's not fair! You always get to do the best things!' said the others, but they knew that it was fair, really.

The children peeked over the railing if they were tall enough, and through it if they weren't, as Alfie held up the boat, said, 'I name this ship the SS *Gone Forever*,' and dropped it into the water. It fluttered down and fell into the water with a tiny splash, and the children rushed to the other side of the bridge to watch it float away.

'It's floating upside down,' said Arthur sniffily.

'It floats just as well as a hat,' said Alfie, and indeed it did. It sailed off, whirling about in the eddies, and eventually disappeared around the bend about two hundred yards away.

'I wonder where it'll end up,' said Sissy, and Alfie replied 'Brazil' in a very wise tone of voice.

On their way home Beryl asked, 'What does "gallivanting" mean? Mr Cramp says it's what we do in holidays if we're not on the harvest.'

'Must be messing about waiting for Dad to come home so we can have tea, then,' said little Albert.

'Must be,' agreed the others.

'What'll we do if Dad finds out what we did?' asked Sissy.

'Run away up the hill,' said Alfie sensibly. 'You know how Dad hates running.'

JIM

The little black-and-tan puppy, with its small bright eyes and wagful rump, grew terribly quickly. He would leap up into the air and lick you on the face quite suddenly when you weren't expecting it, and was very warming indeed on cold evenings if you settled into an armchair with him in your arms. He often slept on Mr Ginger Leghorn's lap after supper, the two of them snoring lightly together.

His most annoying habit was pooping and weeing indoors. The poop smelled much ranker than seemed reasonable for a small dog, and he tended to leave it in just those places where it was hardest to clear up, or most likely to be stepped on. It was not a welcome experience, skidding on dog poop, even in your hobnails. It took five weeks of scolding and being put out in the yard before he realised that if you did it outdoors, you received praise rather than blame, and a biscuit.

His second most annoying habit was diving face first into whatever anyone was trying to do, whether it was homework, or shovelling coal. Everything had to be bitten and worried at. There wasn't much you could do, other than have somebody drag him away and put him out in the yard.

His third most annoying habit was nipping at your hands with his needle-sharp little teeth, leaving punctures in the skin, and sometimes even drawing blood. Arthur Leghorn, bright little boy that he was, suggested, 'Why don't we each carry something that he's actually allowed to chew, and give him that?' He carried a golf ball with a split in the skin, Sissy carried a doll with a missing head, Alfie carried a wooden catapult with one fork broken off, Albert carried an undarnable woollen sock, and Beryl carried a piece of coconut shell. All you had to do was present it to him, saying, 'Here, Jim, have a chew of this!' and he'd be off under the table with it. Of course, you had to remember to fetch it back later, slobber 'n' all.

Equally annoying was his enthusiasm for worrying at your shoes and ankles when you were trying to walk along. Mr Leghorn thought that the only way to deal with this was to keep walking, as if a small demented animal were not attached to his trouser leg at all. The cuffs soon became full of tiny little holes, and many times he accidentally trod on the dog, or was nearly tripped. The children became outraged by the way that Jim kept undoing the laces on their hobnail boots, and would cry out, 'Stop it, Jim! Stop it!' Mrs Leghorn carried a wooden spoon, and would tap him smartly on the haunch if he refused to let go. 'Don't worry,' said Ginger, 'he'll soon grow out of it.' One day he discovered that Jim would lose interest almost straight away if you stopped moving at all, and the whole family adopted the policy of standing stock-still if their ankles were attacked. It was like a game of Grandmother's Footsteps.

When they were not at school, Jim spent all day out with the children, hurtling about on the hillsides and being made to fetch sticks, especially from the pond at the edge of town, where the ducks would scatter as he splashed in. He came and helped with the harvest, chasing futilely after the rabbits that shot out of the ever-diminishing squares in the middle of the fields. He seemed to be a dog that never grew tired, but would abruptly fall asleep when he came home, seeking safety from Tildo under the table, until Mr Ginger Leghorn came home, when he would wake up, go barmy with pleasure and anticipation, and be rewarded with the crusts from Mr Leghorn's lunchtime sandwiches. Mr Leghorn particularly liked the smell behind the dog's ears, and would sniff away at it, saying it was like the combined smell of toast and babies.

The trouble with this dog was that no one could think of a name for him. He came bouncing up, no matter what you called him, and so the children simply called him 'Puppy', or 'Boy', and Molly Leghorn called him 'Nuisance', or 'Piddler', which was not very polite, but she had her reasons, complaining that it was always her and nobody else who had to go and fetch the mop and bucket. He also acquired another name, which came about because, as he grew older, he developed a funny habit of smiling when he was pleased to see you.

This was no ordinary smile. His lips drew back right up to his gums, and his eyes almost closed altogether. If he had not been wagging his tail, you would have thought that he was snarling and just about to give you a nip. 'Gracious me,' said people when they met him, 'I never saw such a grin on a dog in my life!' and so a great many people simply referred to him as 'Grinner', or 'Smiler'.

One evening, at table, Mr Ginger Leghorn said, 'We can't go on having a dog with no name. We've got to think of a moniker.'

'The dog's not bothered,' said Mrs Leghorn.

'Well, I am bothered,' replied Mr Leghorn, 'and the children are bothered, aren't you, children?'

'No,' chorused the children, shaking their heads.

'Let's call it "Dog",' said Albert, who was the smallest, but everybody just ignored him.

'Let's call him "Hobnail",' suggested Arthur.

'Why?' asked Sissy.

'Don't know, really.'

'What about "Lancelot"?' said Beryl.

'Too posh these days,' replied Mr Ginger Leghorn. 'That's even worse than Rupert.'

'I was thinking of the noble knight,' said Beryl, who had been reading *The Tales of the Knights of the Round Table, Retold for Children* by Mrs Humphrey Flopwell, that her mother had given her the previous Christmas.

'What about "Prancelot"?' said Arthur.

'He's not a horse, stupid,' said Sissy.

'Don't call me stupid, stupid.'

'Well, don't be stupid then, stupid.'

'Children! That's enough,' said Molly Leghorn sternly, 'or it'll be early bed without supper for the two of you.'

'Mum, we've already had supper,' pointed out Beryl.

'But you're not in bed yet, are you?' replied her mother.

'What about "Waggalot" or "Barkalot"?' said Alfie.

'What about "Poopalot"?' said Sissy, and the children put their hands to their faces and giggled.

'More like "Guffalot",' said Mr Ginger Leghorn, under his breath, so that no one else would hear him, except that Mrs Molly Leghorn did, and she stuck a sharp elbow into his ribs to reprove him.

'I know what we'll do,' she said. 'We'll tell him to sit, and we'll call him lots of names, and when we get to a name he likes, and wags his tail, that's what we'll call him.'

So that is what they did, and at first it seemed not to work at all. Kneeling around him in a circle, these are the names they tried:

Bertie, Jack, Rover, Teddy, Tony, Bobby, Fido, Caesar, Soldier, Sailor, Danny, Bomber, Buck, Lupo, Lucky, Sam, Tavistock and Exmoor.

The dog wagged his tail pretty much equally at the sound of all of them, and the family was about to give up, when Sissy said 'Jim!' whereupon he leapt into her arms and tried to lick her lips, something she particularly hated because of the slobberiness and the germs. 'Ugh!' she exclaimed, and handed the puppy to Beryl.

'Well, Jim it is,' declared Mr Ginger Leghorn. 'Shall we have a christening?'

He fetched a bottle of ale from the cupboard, pulled the cork, put a finger down into the hole, and dabbed the beer on the dog's forehead. 'I hereby and herewithal, and however and notwithstanding and heretofore above agreed and below appended and all that malarkey, name you "Jim",' he pronounced. 'God bless you and all who sail in you.'

Then he took a swig of the ale, and said, 'Thank God for that. We've got a name at last.'

He plumped himself down into the armchair, said, 'Come on, Jim!' and Jim jumped into his lap.

'Ever since we got the dog, I haven't been on your lap once,' complained Sissy.

'Well, you're not very restful,' said Mr Ginger Leghorn. 'Jim only bites my fingers. He doesn't pinch my nose or pull my ears or tug at both ends of my moustache at the same time, or try to make funny shapes with my lips.'

JIM AND TILDO

Tildo the fluffy cat was still not at all pleased about Jim's arrival in the house, and got into the habit of stalking up to him, all his fur standing on end to make himself look bigger, baring his teeth and hissing, and swiping him across the nose, as if to say, 'I was here first, this is my territory, and you'd better leave before I do something a lot worse.'

Poor Jim would yelp and creep away, his tail between his legs, with dark blood purling out of the tracks across his snout, and Mrs Molly Leghorn would shoo Tildo out, saying, 'Horrid cat! How could you be so nasty to such a nice little puppy? What did he ever do to you?' Tildo would go and sit on the windowsill outside the kitchen, glaring down through the glass at the dog, who would look up, whimper, and go back to hide under the kitchen table, where he now had a tattered old army blanket that Mr Ginger Leghorn had cadged from the quartermaster of his yeomanry regiment.

It did not seem to matter how much Jim wanted to be friends with Tildo, the cat still hissed at him and took a swipe at his nose. Everyone could see that Jim desperately wanted to be friends, but Tildo would not be mollified.

After about a month, when Jim had grown quite a lot, and the first breaths of autumn were in the air, there came a day when Tildo forgot to scratch the dog. He walked straight past with his tail up, and took no notice as he headed for the back door with his mind empty of dogs, but furbished with mice and rats instead.

Jim cringed and whimpered and ran under the table, and then realised that something was wrong. It took a little time to work it out, but then he saw that he had nothing to cringe or whimper about. This was certainly most peculiar. He crept out again, and went to the back door to watch Tildo going up the hill. He decided to follow, but thought better of it when Tildo turned and looked at him with his big yellow eyes.

The next day, Tildo again forgot to scratch the puppy, or even hiss at it, but padded off past him, out of the door and up the hill, thinking of rabbits.

On the day after that Tildo absent-mindedly bumped Jim under the chin as he passed him on the way to the back door, and the day after that Tildo went round and round his legs in figures of eight, and bumped him under the chin a great many times. Jim just stood there in confusion wondering what this could all possibly mean.

The day after that Jim absent-mindedly sniffed at Tildo's backside because he had momentarily forgotten that Tildo wasn't a dog, and Tildo hurried away to get that cold nose away from his bottom.

And then there came the day when the children came in at five o'clock with empty stomachs and grubby faces and knees, and Sissy and Albert knelt down to look under the table to see if Jim was there in his usual place. 'Blimey,' said Albert, and whispered to the other children. 'Here, you lot, come and look at this! Mum, come and look at this!'

Down on their knees, they all saw the puppy fast asleep, with Tildo perched on top of him like a tea cosy. Tildo stared back at them with his big insolent yellow eyes, as if to say 'What's the matter with you lot? Never seen a cat with a dog before?'

It wasn't long after that when a bad-tempered brindled dog picked on Jim out in the street. Jim had never been in a proper dogfight before, and had no idea what to do if a big growly stranger suddenly grabs one of your ears in its teeth and tries to pull it off. He attempted to roll over and surrender, but it was difficult with one ear in such painful captivity, so he squeaked and yelped instead. Luckily, Tildo had been at the windowsill watching life out in the street, and suddenly there was a streak of tabby-coloured fluff, as he shot out of the door and hurled himself at the brindled dog, knocked it over sideways, and raked it across the eyes and snout with his claws. The dog let go of Jim's ear, leapt to its feet, and hurtled off down the street with its tail between its legs, and Tildo in hot pursuit.

Like Mr Ginger Leghorn, cats are not fond of running for any length of time, so Tildo was soon back, bumping Jim under the chin with the top of his head.

The neighbours who had witnessed it all relayed the news to the Leghorn family, and Mr Ginger Leghorn gave Beryl sixpence to go to the butcher's and come back with a marrowbone for Jim, and a little piece of ox liver for Tildo.

BUCKETS AND CHAIR LEGS

It is true that all puppies are charming and entertaining, and so to say that Jim had both those qualities does not tell anyone anything at all surprising.

Some puppies, however, are a little bit like people who show signs of eccentricity from an early age.

Jim's first curious obsession was that he started to hate the sound of a chair being scraped across the flagstones of the kitchen. He found it extremely annoying and outrageous. Dogs have better hearing than humans, and perhaps he could hear something we cannot, such as a very high-pitched, painful squeak.

Whatever it was, that scraping sound made him so angry that he had no choice but to attack the chair concerned. He would leap up, furious and snarling (which always made Tildo fly for the door), and throw himself at whichever chair leg first presented itself for savaging. Sometimes it was difficult to wrestle the chair away from him if you wanted to sit down again, because Jim would simply not let go unless you said

'Bucket, Jim!', and you'll find out why that worked in just a moment.

The children, of course, scraped their chairs on purpose, and Mr and Mrs Leghorn lifted their chairs carefully to avoid making any scraping noise at all.

After a while the chair legs began to look very sorry indeed, all ragged and chewed and punctured, and of course Tildo made it all much worse by using them as scratching posts.

At this point Mr and Mrs Leghorn had to decide whether to get new chairs and keep the animals away from them, or put up with the continuing damage. It was not a difficult decision. New ones were expensive, and anyway the whole family enjoyed it when Jim attacked the chairs, and they weren't going to give it up just for the sake of smartness.

And now for the bucket story: Mrs Molly Leghorn had a galvanised bucket with a special grid on one side for squeezing out a mop, and Jim loved it when she was mopping the kitchen floor. He would pounce on the mop-head and cling on to it with his teeth so that the only way she could get on with mopping was to swing the puppy around the floor. Normally she would shut Jim out of the house and do the mopping, but quite often, just to enter-tain visitors, she would show them her dogmop in action.

Jim loved the laughter and applause, and this only made him worse, so sometimes he would go to the corner and bark at the mop and bucket until somebody got them out and had to pretend to clean the floor so that he could be swung around. The floor became very shiny, and Jim became very grimy, and every few days he would have to be washed in the garden, which he also loved, because at the end he would shake all the water from his body, and whoever was washing him would have to run out of the way of the shining shower of drops. The children enjoyed avoiding Jim's showers.

It happened that one day nobody was paying atten-tion to his barking at the mop and bucket, so he thought he would take urgent action to remedy the situation. He picked the bucket up by the rim, which must have felt quite strange to his teeth, and tried to carry it into the parlour, where Mrs Molly Leghorn was having a cup of tea, and a break from the mangle.

The trouble was that he could not see where he was going with the big bucket right in front of his eyes. He clanged into the table leg, and then clanged into the leg next to it. He clanged into the cupboard under the sink and then clanged into the door jamb.

Mrs Molly Leghorn heard the mysterious clanging coming her way, but knew it was not the ghost of a long-dead knight with his head under his arm, because along with the clanging there was a sort of muffled and echoey barking and growling.

'Oh, Jim! You daft puppy!' she cried, as the dog came into the parlour and clanged straight into her. Jim put the bucket down, backed off, and started barking at it.

'I don't want to do any mopping,' she said.

Jim went back to the kitchen to fetch the mop. It was all very well, but he couldn't get it through the doorway when he held it in the middle, and it didn't occur to him to drag it along lengthways by the mop end, so he just carried on trying to get it through the doorway while Mrs Leghorn stood there laughing at him. So he dropped the mop and returned to his bucket. He clanged into the doorways and walls before he dropped it at Mrs Leghorn's feet.

Jim loved the patting and hugging he got from Mrs Leghorn as she laughed at him, and, being a natural entertainer, he repeated the bucket trick the next day, and again when the children and Mr Leghorn came home. Their delight was wonderful to him, and even more wonderful was the big digestive biscuit that Alfie gave him as a reward.

That was the fatal move. In dog mathematics it meant bucket = biscuit. If anyone said 'Bucket, Jim!' it was pretty much the same as anyone saying 'Biscuit!'

The odd thing is that because the bucket was so heavy, not only did Jim develop a very strong neck and jaws, but the tips of his sharp white teeth began to go blunt. When Arthur told Mr Ginger Leghorn about it, he prised open the dog's mouth, had a look, and said, 'That's bad news, that is! What if he gets in a fight and can't look after himself?'

So Mr Leghorn went out and came back from the ironmonger's with a much smaller galvanised iron bucket. Around the rim he tied the sleeves of an old shirt. He got some contact glue and painted it all around the inside rim, and stuck on a nice wide strip of thick black rubber made of an old inner tube.

Fortunately Jim much preferred this bucket. When you woofed into it, it made a higher note than the big bucket, and you could carry it around, bumping into things, for very much longer. He soon discovered that it was less like hard work if, instead of holding the bucket in his jaws, he just inserted his whole head into it and wore it like a helmet.

People used to call round on the Leghorns just to see Jim clanging into things with his bucket on his head, and he even made the local paper. There was a lovely photograph in it of the whole family standing proudly behind, with Jim sitting in front, bucket on head. The caption read: 'Meet Grinner the Local Dogmop, Master of Comedy. We Love Him, Say Family.'

JIM AND SNIFFY

Once, when Christmas was not too far away, Jim went missing and was not seen for two days.

Mrs Molly Leghorn grew more and more distraught, as did Mr Ginger Leghorn and the children. Over and over again, Mrs Molly Leghorn would say, 'Oh, I'm sure he's just out having an adventure, I'm sure he'll be back soon,' but she did not really believe it, and neither did Mr Ginger Leghorn when he replied, 'Course he will. Dogs are always wandering off, aren't they? You can't just keep them locked in the house all day. It's not natural, is it?'

The children were upset and tearful, and Tildo was wandering about making that special miaow that cats have when they are looking for their kittens.

On the third day, Mrs Molly Leghorn said, 'Something's happened to him, hasn't it? I just know it has. What are we going to do?'

Mr Ginger Leghorn put a card up in the post office saying

Has enywon seen our dog Jim? He is medjum small and

black an tan and has been missin three days. Please reply to
Number 4 Railway Cottiges.

The children went up and down the street knocking on doors and asking if anyone had seen Jim, but nobody had. They came home with heavy hearts, and little Sissy and Albert were both crying.

'What about that acker of yours with the tracker dog?' suggested Mrs Molly Leghorn to her husband.

'What? Smiffy and Sniffy?'

'Yes, those two. I bet they could find him.'

'You're brilliant,' said Mr Ginger Leghorn, and kissed her on the cheek.

'Oh, don't,' she said, 'I'm a respectable married woman, I am.'

Mr Ginger Leghorn put on his bicycle clips, took a hurricane lamp and set off on his bicycle for Smiffy's house, which was two miles away in the countryside just outside of town.

Smiffy was a blacksmith and farrier who could make almost anything in metal, and was known to have a great way with horses. When he worked at night you could see the sparks ascending prettily into the air above his house, almost like Roman candles. He lived alone, and on the evening that Mr Ginger Leghorn arrived, he was frying chops above the charcoal of his brazier because there did not seem to be any point in lighting a stove in the kitchen when you already had a perfect fire out in the forge. He had a large potato wrapped in clay, cooking at the front end of the furnace, where it was not too hot. In the winter Smiffy sometimes slept in the forge, to take advantage of the lingering heat. He lived most of his life in an orange glow, wearing not much more than a thick leather apron, covered in soot and grime, and as happy as any man could ask. The only time he was ever smartly dressed was when he went out with the yeomanry, along with his friend Mr Ginger Leghorn. On those days he would set up a big galvanised bath, fill it with water heated on the brazier, and he would emerge from it looking clean and handsome indeed.

Smiffy's dog was a bloodhound, a big floppy sad-eyed animal with long droopy ears and big paws, and it could find anything just about anywhere once it had caught a whiff of whatever it was after. When he was looking for something he would put his head up and do 'belling', which is the name for the very musical and mournful howling that is a bloodhound speciality, and which they particularly enjoy. His name was Sniffy, of course, and he was quite often borrowed by the local police for their occasional searches for missing people and escaped convicts who had fled across the moor.

When Mr Ginger Leghorn had explained his problem, Smiffy agreed that he and Sniffy would call round at the railway cottage in the morning. Mr Ginger Leghorn would be at work, and the children at school, but Mrs Molly Leghorn would be there, doing some of the washing that she had taken in. She used the mangle when the children were out, because they liked to pretend to put their fingers into it, and it nearly always gave her kittens.

In the morning Smiffy gave Sniffy a good smell of Jim's old army blanket, and said 'Good boy, Sniffy! Go seek!' and Sniffy put his nose to the ground and set off straight out of the back door. He went to the fence and sniffed at a gap under it, so Smiffy opened the gate and called Sniffy through. Sniffy quartered the ground, and then set off up the hillside. He went round the hill, down it, and then back up, and then stopped at a large hole, where he belled very majestically before putting his nose back to the hole and testing it with some very delicate sniffs. Then he belled again.

'Good boy,' said Smiffy. 'Now you wait here. Stay! Do you hear me? Stay! I'm off to get a spade. Back in a mo.'

Smiffy trotted off and returned breathlessly some ten minutes later, with Mr Leghorn's spade over his shoulder. Sniffy lay down and relaxed, watching Smiffy digging away at the hole, and occasionally sniffing to see what else was going on in the world.

Smiffy found Jim's backside some four feet down, and after some careful digging with the spade and then with his hands, he pulled Jim out.

Jim was in a terrible state and hardly responded at all. It was not hunger, but thirst that had almost killed him, and he was barely conscious. Smiffy abandoned the spade, thinking he would come back for it later, and put Jim round his shoulders rather in the way that the Good Shepherd carries a sheep in the illustrated Bibles that people used to have in those days. 'Come on, Sniffy,' he said to his dog. 'Let's get this little blighter back home! And don't you get the idea to go digging.'

Sniffy got to his feet and followed his master, thinking aromatic bloodhound thoughts that were infinitely beyond the olfactory understanding of humans. Smiffy left a note for Mrs Leghorn on her kitchen table: *Sniffy found him all right, but he's in a state. Got him at mine.* When she came home with a pat of butter from the corner shop, she saw the note and bicycled round to Smiffy's forge.

When she got there, Mrs Leghorn looked at the young dog in dismay. He was half dead. She and Mr Leghorn were not exactly poor, but they were not rich enough to afford a vet either. Between them they earned just about enough to keep going, with one day trip on a charabanc every year.

'He's got no light in his eyes!' she exclaimed. 'He's going to die, isn't he?'

'Don't cry,' said Smiffy. 'It's thirst. If you think about it, he's had nothing for nearly three days now.'

Mrs Molly Leghorn had a brainwave, and went home and fetched the cake-icing syringe from her kitchen drawer. She put the nozzle into a bowl of water from the pump, and sucked it in. Smiffy opened Jim's mouth gently, and Mrs Leghorn squirted the water down the back of his gullet. She did it several times, and Jim seemed to perk up quite quickly.

'Better not do too much at once, missus,' said Smiffy. 'I've heard it's best to take it slowly. Least, that's what they tell us in the yeomanry.'

'Well, you can kill with kindness, that's for sure,' said Mrs Molly Leghorn.

Smiffy picked Jim off the table and tried to set him on his feet. 'Not quite ready yet,' he said, putting him back on the table.

But by the time Mr Ginger Leghorn returned that evening, Jim was definitely ready, and was back at home. He had eaten some lights from the butcher, and some stale bread soaked in milk, and was fast asleep under the table with Tildo perched on top of him, in his usual place.

Mr Leghorn took a marrowbone round for Sniffy, and a big pipkin of home-brewed beer for Smiffy, which he helped him to drink before he wobbled slowly home again on his bicycle.

Mr Ginger Leghorn said, 'Well, it just goes to show what happens when you haven't a proper job of work to do. If you're a dog you end up down a bunny hole, and if you're a man you end up drunk on a bench, or thieving, or something, and if you're a woman you spend all day in bed. That dog's got to have a proper job.'

'A proper job? Like Sniffy?' said Mrs Molly Leghorn. 'But what could Jim do?'

'I've thought of one already,' said Mr Leghorn.

'Tildo hasn't got a proper job,' said Sissy.

'Yes he has,' replied her father. 'He's self-employed, and half the time we don't know what he's doing at all. It's like being a spy. Top secret.'

JIM'S NEW JOB

Ginger Leghorn gave Jim a good brushing, and fastened the collar and box around his neck. Jim whined and worried at it with his paw, but Ginger pushed it downwards, said 'Good dog', and gave him a biscuit. Very soon Jim realised that if he put up with the box, he would get biscuits. In dog mathematics, in other words, box = biscuits.

After Jim had become used to the box, Ginger trained Jim to shake hands. He would make him sit, say 'Paw!' and lean down and lift Jim's right paw with his hand. He would hold it for a few seconds, and give him a little corner of biscuit. Sometimes Ginger would say 'Shake hands!' and perform the same manoeuvre, and sometimes he would say 'Say please!' until Jim realised that paw = shake hands = say please = biscuits. Naturally, Jim would adopt a pleading expression without any training at all.

The truly difficult job was training Jim to bark a soft thank-you when he was given a coin. It was easy when he was given a biscuit instead. Mr Leghorn spent many hours on his hands and knees in front of Jim, with a box hanging around his neck, barking as the children repeatedly presented him with a coin. The dog found this very entertaining, but never got the message, so, in the end, Mr Leghorn gave up, saying, 'Well, you can't have everything. Can you?'

One morning Mr Ginger Leghorn called Jim and fastened the collar and box around his neck. 'Say goodbye to Jim,' he said to the children, and they patted him on the head and said, 'Have a good day at work, Jim. See you later, Dad.'

'Toodleoo, my nitty little ankle-biters,' said Ginger. 'See you later. Come along, Jim!'

So, watched by Tildo from the windowsill, and waved off by the family, Jim and Ginger went down to the railway station to catch the 7.20.

Many of the locomotives had to stop for several minutes at the station in order to take on coal or water, and so, when the 7.20 stopped, Ginger and Jim got into a carriage and began to work their way along.

You can always tell if someone likes dogs. They hold out a hand for the dog to sniff, or they say something a little stupid like 'Who's a lovely boy then?' or they say 'I used to have a dog a bit like that, and do you know what he used to do?' In a word, it is very easy to find out who might feel like giving a dog a coin for his collection box, and who can resist a brown-eyed dog who holds up his paw to say 'please'?

Jim's first contributors were Mr and Mrs Hamilton McCosh of Eltham, a handsome Scottish couple who were travelling first class to play a week's golf at Trevose Head. He gave Jim a half-crown, and she gave him a florin. They had a large and badly behaved dog with them, appropriately called Bouncer, who wanted to play with Jim, causing such a kerfuffle that Ginger had to drag Jim out before he was squashed. Sadly, this inaugural generosity of the McCoshes was not often matched by subsequent donors, not many of whom were speculators who had just had a windfall.

Almost everybody loved the black-and-tan dog with the Railway Widows and Orphans Fund collecting box around his neck, and were touched when Ginger said 'Say please, Jim' and the dog put up his right paw. Most were happy to shake his paw and put a few coppers, or just a farthing, in the collection box. Jim and Ginger collected a shilling's worth in the second carriage they tried. After that, they just had enough time to work another carriage, and got ninepence halfpenny. Some people even gave Jim a little corner of their sandwich, or a broken biscuit from their handbag, but before long Jim became contented with a pat on the head or a good ruffling of the ears. He quickly grew to love his new job.

The Railway Widows and Orphans Fund was Ginger Leghorn's favourite charity. In fact it was the favourite charity of all the railwaymen, because there was such a terrible need for it. In those times people died of all sorts of horrible diseases that are easily cured these days, and besides, on the railways, there were a great many fatal accidents. There were more train crashes, and you might easily fall out of a train because you could open the doors while it was still moving, and sometimes the doors even fell open on their own. People could get buried under heaps of coal, and quite often the men working on the tracks would get hit. Life was very insecure, all the way round, and this meant that someone had to look after the poor families that were left behind with no money. All over the country, there were dogs like Jim who collected contributions from passengers, and they were, quite coincidentally, very often known as 'Station Jim'. Sometimes they travelled with the guard, and sometimes they lived at a station, and hopped on and off the trains when they were waiting for passengers to get on or disembark.

The great aim for the Railway Widows and Orphans Fund dogs was that they should learn to work the carriages on their own, thus freeing their owners to do their jobs. Ginger Leghorn was assistant stationmaster, and could not really spare much time for leading Jim through the carriages, so before long he was putting Jim in through the door at the front end of a carriage, and calling him out through the door at the other end when the train was ready to leave. Ginger would put his hand under Jim's box to see how heavy it was getting, and every now and then he would take it into the stationmaster's office and empty it out into the big collection box that they had there.

Occasionally there would be a horrible person who would shoo Jim away, or even take a kick at him, but for the most part he became very popular with the passengers, who loved his extraordinary grin, and would become worried if he was not there. Jim became really a little too fat from all the snacks he was given, and in the holidays Ginger would usually leave him at home so that the children could play with him up on the hillside, and get him fit again. Ginger thought it was cruel to deprive Jim and the children of each other's company at holiday time.

Sometimes Jim travelled all day in the guard's van, among the bicycles, trunks, mailbags and sets of golf clubs, and came to know all the branch lines and little country stations that we used to have. Somehow his itinerary was always worked out so that he returned before it was too late, and found his own way home, laden down with coins, when he would whine and scratch at the door to be let in, so that Ginger had to screw a large brass plate across it to protect the paintwork.

Many of the guards had their own cats who kept them company in their van, and those were the ones where Jim was never to be found, because although he was respectful and affectionate with Tildo, he was very much less considerate of other cats, and a spat with a cat is an alarming thing on a train in motion.

Before long Jim was known all over the GWR, whose employees were so proud of it that they called it 'God's Wonderful Railway'.

The odd thing was, that when people did present Jim with a coin, he soon began the habit of giving a small woof of appreciation, and everybody said, 'What a polite dog.'

THE POSTMAN'S LEG

Just down the road from the Leghorns' house was an old pub that had been a coaching inn for two hundred years. Here the carriages would arrive to change horses for the next leg of their journey, and passengers would alight or get off. There were iron rings set into the walls and door-posts so that people could tether their horses, and there was a stone trough donated by the Drinking Troughs for Animals Society. Inscribed around the rim in Gothic lettering were the words *For Kindness' Sake, Let the Dogs and Horses Drink, and the Lord Shall Reward You, For They Are Our Brothers and Sisters.*

At the centre of the courtyard stood a tall and stout post, and this is where Bonaparte the pub dog had his kennel. He was called Bonaparte because he was so big and strong that he could have pulled your bones apart if he had wanted to. He was a mastiff; his head was enormous, his jaws were like gin traps, his chest was broad and his legs rippled with muscle. In Britain and Ireland you don't often see dogs as big and powerful as this any more, but if you were to go to Turkey you would see them out in the countryside, guarding the sheep. In the days when wolves were a danger, these dogs would wear iron collars with long spikes, so that no wolf could take them by the throat. The Turkish shepherd dogs are light grey and black, and Bonaparte was the same size, but brindled like a boxer. Like a boxer, his fur was shiny and short.

Bonaparte, despite his fearsome size, was a very gentle and well-liked dog. In his own mind his job was to meet and greet visitors, which he always did with great joyfulness, even if he had never met them before. It was quite something to have a huge pair of paws descend on your shoulders, to have your face licked by an enormous slobbery pink tongue, and be breathed on by truly fetid dog-breath.

The landlord of the pub thought that Bonaparte's job was to be an especially intimidating guard dog, and it is true that at night his great deep voice would set to belling in the event of anything worrying, such as a fox coughing in the distance, or someone calling in their cat. Otherwise he would growl in his sleep as he dreamed of epic ancestral battles with other gigantic dogs, and men with axes and matted beards.

Station Jim and Bonaparte were quite good friends, because Mr Ginger Leghorn liked to go and drink at the pub on the evenings when he was not on duty at the station. Jim did not seem to mind being completely flattened by Bonaparte as they romped in the yard, and sometimes they fell asleep on their sides, with Jim tucked up like a Russian doll, in between Bonaparte's legs, and up against his belly. All it needed was a corgi to make a set of three.

Because Bonaparte was a popular dog, as well as a local wonder who attracted visitors in his own right, some people used to bring him presents of postmen's legs. These were in fact the leg bones of cows, and you could pick them up for a few pennies at the butcher's.

Station Jim also liked postmen's legs. They would arrive all shiny and white, apart from the lovely bits of gristly meat that were still attached to them. He got a postman's leg every Christmas, to get him outdoors while the children opened their presents.

One day Bonaparte had been disrespectful. He had tried to embrace the Mayor, so he had been tethered on a chain to the big stout post in the courtyard until such time as that very important and worthy gentleman had finished his pint of porter and departed. Poor Bonaparte was having a frustrating time meeting and greeting the customers because even he could not go beyond the length of the chain that held him captive. He had been reduced to lying on the ground, sighing, and raising his eyebrows alternately.

Then, luckily for him, the butcher came by in his cart, called out 'Here, Boney! Catch!' and tossed him a magnificent postman's leg. Bonaparte pinned it down with one forepaw, and set about killing it all over again, savaging it and shaking his head from side to side. The sight of that would have been enough to deter any intruder.

Bonaparte's luck was short-lived, however, because Ginger Leghorn turned up with Station Jim, who was still wearing his collecting box.

Normally, Bonaparte would have been delighted to see Jim, and they would have frolicked together in the courtyard, but on this occasion he was not remotely pleased. Not only was he chained up, which made him feel vulnerable, but he had a postman's leg to defend. He was not a dog who had any generous notions about how nice it was to share your food with friends. When Jim trotted up to him, he rose to his full height, placed one vast paw on the bone, bared his teeth and snarled.

Jim was mystified. Why had his friend so suddenly turned against him? But then he smelled the bone, made his eyes follow his nose, and spotted it, safely in Bonaparte's custody, under that stupendous paw. The mystery was over; Station Jim did not believe in sharing his food either, and all this snarling and growling and menacing struck him as perfectly reasonable. Even so, he sat down and thought the situation over. It would, after all, be rather nice to get his own jaws around that postman's leg.

Ten minutes later, Ginger Leghorn and the other inmates of the coaching inn heard a powerful and mournful howling from out in the yard. Only one hound in the whole district would have been capable of howling as loudly and mournfully as that, with the possible exception of Sniffy the Bloodhound. 'What's up with Boney?' they said, taking another sip, and looking at each other. Ginger stood up and looked out of the window. 'Well, I'll be blowed,' he said.

Station Jim had been busy. He had kept himself out of reach of Bonaparte, and at just the point when the mastiff was concentrating on a particularly threatening growl,

Station Jim had nipped in and pinched the bone. Then, and this is the intelligent part, he had teased Bonaparte by staying just out of his reach, and walking in a circle.

What Ginger had seen was Bonaparte up against the post, with his chain wrapped round it, howling, while his little friend settled down to a good gnaw and gnash on the postman's leg, safely out of reach. Bonaparte could think of nothing but to go into a deep despair, his world having suddenly become a dark and tragic place.

Ginger went out and stood sternly over his dog. 'You are a very bad boy,' he said.

Jim looked up with a 'What? Me?' expression, and Ginger said, 'Drop! Drop it at once!'

This time the expression said 'What? Really? Are you serious?'

'Drop it, or I will give you what for,' said Ginger.

Jim dropped it reluctantly, and backed off, with his own deep sense of tragedy growing in his heart. Ginger bent down to pick it up, even though it was disgustingly slobbery. He thought of giving it back by hand, but wondered if Bonaparte would remove it gently enough not to take his fingers off, so he tossed it to the dog's feet. Happiness flooded back into Bonaparte's heart, the universe settled back into a just and rational order, and he settled down to resume the destruction of the bone.

'You're a bad dog,' said Ginger, as he put Jim's lead on, but if Jim had been able to think in words, he would have been thinking, 'Yes, but I am a very clever dog, and I have just experienced a great moment of glory, and several minutes of profound personal happiness.'

STATION JIM'S CHRISTMAS

Once upon a time, in the year 1714, there was a German aristocrat who became King of England, Scotland, Wales and Ireland. By not being able to speak a word of English he accidentally created our modern democratic political system, because he had to leave all the discussions and decisions to a group of ministers called the Cabinet, with a prime minister in charge. 'Cabinet' is an old-fashioned French word for 'toilet', but it also means a kind of box. Possibly the ministers met in a toilet, or in a box, who knows. Perhaps the ministers had to stand around while the Prime Minister got to be the only one to sit on the toilet. No wonder the King never showed up.

More importantly, if you love your food, the new King brought with him a kind of pudding that you could make without meat. Perhaps you didn't know that puddings were originally made inside an animal's stomach, but after the animal was dead, of course. To this day in Scotland, a sheep's stomach is used for making haggis, and that is a proper old-fashioned pudding.

King George's pudding was made by being squished tightly into a cloth, tied up and steamed.

One Sunday Mrs Molly Leghorn was conversing with her neighbours on the subject of puddings, and there was some confusion about which Sunday was going to be the last Sunday before the first Sunday of Advent. There are four Sundays in Advent, which are the four before Christmas, so for Molly and her friends the truly important question was 'Which is the fifth Sunday before Christmas? Is it this one?'

Molly had already made a pound of breadcrumbs, and shelled and chopped the Brazil nuts, and blanched and skinned and chopped the almonds, and grated the cooking apples, and grated a lemon rind and squeezed out the juice, and stoned and chopped the dates, and bought some eggs and some demerara sugar and a little bottle of rum, and weighed out some sultanas and currants, and a little posset of mixed spices, and had even bought some green bananas. Most important of all, she had saved up nine silver threepences, one for each of the humans, and one each for Tildo and Station Jim.

'I know what,' said Mrs Draggit from next door, 'one of us should pop into church, and report back.'

'I always go anyway,' said Mrs Molly Leghorn, who loved the hymns, enjoyed being dressed up in her Sunday best, liked to take a look at the other women's hats, and wanted to keep on the right side of God just in case there really was a Hell hereafter. 'I'll tell you when I come out. I'll send one of the nippers round.'

'You do that,' said Mrs Draggit. 'I've got to stay at home and do the roast, or there'll be hell from his lordship when he reels in from the you-know-what.'

Accordingly, when she heard the bell begin to ring, Mrs Molly Leghorn set off up the hill to the rather grand church, and settled in a pew as far away as possible from Mrs Middle, a very large lady who was married to a fisherman, stank of fish, seldom washed, ate a great many raw onions, and snored loudly through the services from start to finish.

Mrs Middle's capacity for sleeping through the services was often remarked upon, for the Reverend William 'Boomer' Crisp-Blethering was partially deaf, and had no idea how loud was his own voice. He boomed through his sermons and prayers like Gabriel summoning the dead on the Last Day, but without the trumpets. There was also something hypnotic about his immense red beard, the forests of hair sprouting out of his ears, his vermilion lips, and his intense blue eyes; it was impossible to take your eyes off him, unless you were Mrs Middle, fast asleep and oblivious in the front pew, with her chin almost in her lap.

There is in the service a little item called the Collect, which is somewhat like a little extra prayer that seems to have been thrown in for luck, much as a greengrocer might give you an extra plum as well as the pound of quinces that you asked for.

This is what Mrs Molly Leghorn and the congregation (apart from Mrs Middle) were waiting for:

'Stir up, we beseech thee, O Lord, the wills of thy faithful people; that they, plenteously bringing forth the fruit of good works, may of thee be plenteously rewarded.'

On this Sunday, the ladies of the congregation heard these words boomed out by the redoubtable Reverend William 'Boomer' Crisp-Blethering, and lifted their heads like athletes at the beginning of the countdown. Old cavalrymen were reminded of the snorting and bridling of their chargers at the sound of the bugle as they formed up in line abreast at the commencement of battle.

When Mrs Molly Leghorn got home, she sent the children off in different directions with the message: 'Ma says it's Stir-up Sunday 'cause she heard old Boomer say it in the collection.'

After church, and into the afternoon, the Ginger Leghorns made Christmas pudding. Every one of the family, apart from the two animals, made a wish as they stirred the mixture from east to west, in memory of the journey of the Magi. Alfie wished for snow on Christmas Day. Arthur wished for a piece of shortbread. Beryl wished for a proper new pair of shoes instead of the terrible old cobbled-up pair of hobnails she had inherited from another family. Sissy wished for a new kitten. Albert wished for a grey pet rabbit with lop-ears and a twitchy nose. Mrs Molly Leghorn wished for a hat like Mrs Middle's, with artificial flowers in the band, and Mr Ginger Leghorn wished for a pay rise. Grinner the dog would have wished for a postman's leg, if only he had known, and oddly enough, Tildo the cat would also have wished for a rabbit.

When everybody had had a stir, Mrs Molly Leghorn bound up the pudding in an old tea cloth, and put the handle of a wooden spoon through the knot. She took the kettle from the top of the wood burner, where it had been singing away in anticipation of an infinity of pots of tea, and replaced it with a large saucepan. She poured the water from the kettle into it, and set the pudding to hang above, covering the whole thing loosely with a lid so that not too much steam was lost. The lid rattled for hours, and whenever the music of it slowed down, everybody knew it was time to put in more water. Last year Mrs Molly Leghorn had left her husband in charge, and he had gone out to fetch more coal from the station and allowed the bottom of the pan to burn out and wreck the pudding. This was the nearest that Mrs Molly Leghorn had ever come to demanding a divorce.

Just as it was beginning to get dark outside, she lit the lamps and took the pudding off the steam. On Christmas Day she would install the silver threepenny bits at even intervals, to make sure that everybody had one, and she would make Camperdown sauce, which she had learned from one of her friends who had once been the servant of a don of Clare College in Cambridge. Everybody loved Mrs Molly Leghorn's Camperdown sauce, which, with her fingers crossed behind her back, she liked to say was fantastically complicated and difficult to make. The hard work was always left to Alfie and Arthur, who took it in turns to whip the butter and sugar together until they had gone beyond fluffiness and the mixture was almost running.

That evening there was the usual quarrel about what to eat on Christmas Day. 'Well, shall we have sheep's tongue, a boar's head or a goose?' asked Mrs Leghorn, and as always Mr Ginger Leghorn said, 'A boar's head. It's more traditional, i'n't it?'

'Oh but, Dad,' cried Beryl, 'it's so horrid having a big fat face on the table and then watching it all being cut up!'

'You get used to it,' said her father. 'And it's got a big Bramley in its mouth, and that's really nice. And we can give the bones to Jim.'

'I want sheep's tongue!' cried Alfie, banging the table with his fist.

'No you don't,' said Sissy. 'Tongue's disgusting. You're only saying that to be a noisy nuisance.'

'A noisy noise annoys a noisy oyster,' chanted Albert.

'A noisier noise annoys a noisy oyster more,' chanted Beryl.

'The noisiest noise annoys a noisy oyster most,' said Mr Ginger Leghorn.

'Come on, what are we going to have?' demanded Mrs Leghorn.

'Let's have a vote,' said Beryl. 'Who votes for sheep's tongue?'

Alfie put up his hand.

'And who votes for boar's head?'

Mr Ginger Leghorn put his hand up.

'And who wants goose?'

Everybody except Mr Ginger Leghorn and Alfie put up their hands.

'You're overruled,' said Mr Ginger Leghorn. 'I'm in charge around here. We're having a boar's head. If I'm paying for it out of my hard-earned wages, that's what we're having.'

'You may think you're in charge,' said his wife, 'but I'm the cook, and I say we're having goose, because the grease is perfect for roast potatoes. And that's that. And I'll stuff it with chestnut, pork and apple, and we'll have bread sauce.'

'What about boar's head next year?' asked Ginger forlornly.

'Well, are you offering to cook it?'

'If you show me how.'

'Not on your nelly,' said Mrs Leghorn. 'I'm not having you galumphing about in my kitchen with your filthy fingernails and your dropping things on the floor and putting them back in the dish, and helping yourself to girt mouthfuls before anything's even got to the table, and you licking your fingers. Alfie, be a dear, and tomorrow after school you run down to the farm and ask them for a big goose to be collected on the 23rd, and I'll give you half a crown to give Mr Major for a deposit.'

'Can we all go?' asked Sissy.

'Safety in numbers,' said Mr Leghorn. 'But don't take the dog. He'll set to chasing the ducks and chickens and being a bloody nuisance.'

In the days that followed, the orange box full of Christmas decorations was retrieved from the cupboard under the stairs and the ones that were too worn out or mouse-eaten were thrown on the fire. Alfie and Arthur and Beryl and Jim went out into the woods between Lady Huffington's house and the railway line, to collect strands of ivy and small branches of yew and laurel. They found a holly tree covered in red berries, and brought home some sprigs of that too. Best of all, Alfie spotted some mistletoe a long way up a very high tree, and climbed all the way there with the kitchen scissors in his mouth, like a pirate raiding a ship with his cutlass between his teeth. It was the bravest thing he had ever done, and his heart was pounding all the way up, but when he finally came down and thumped back to earth, he puffed out his chest and swaggered confidently as if it had all been a doddle.

Back in the railway cottage, Molly Leghorn and the little ones tied gold ribbon into bows and stuck them everywhere they could think of on the walls and doors. Sissy cut out new stars from cardboard, and glued onto them the gold foil from Ginger's cigarette packets, which they had been saving for weeks. Albert cut out rectangles of cardboard for the others to make Christmas cards, but he drew nothing himself because he knew he was a terrible artist, and Beryl would do it so much better, with her swirly and squiggly handwriting that was like no one else's and that had not apparently been learned from anyone. She knew how to make little pictures out of scraps of cloth, and she even knew how to make the glue out of flour and water.

Sissy helped her mother make peppermints and sugared almonds to give away as presents, and after the children were in bed, Molly Leghorn lovingly embroidered with their names a handkerchief for each of her children. She did it so beautifully that they never got used, and there they remained, forever pristine, smelling faintly of lavender, in the drawers where the children's clothes were kept.

The children were sent in all directions to deliver the Christmas cards by hand, and were often lucky enough to be rewarded with a toffee or a stick of liquorice, or a humbug. Jim came along too, hoping for morsels of biscuit, and straining at the leash at each glimpse of a cat. Mrs Leghorn knew that the more cards you sent out, the more you received in return, and it was her ambition, one of these Christmases, to get so many that there would hardly be a surface in the house that was not covered with them.

Best of all was the singing around the piano by lamplight in the many houses of those who had them, with the coals glowing ardently in the fireplaces, and the aroma of strange family drinks, such as Mrs Lilly Posnett's mulled cider boosted with sherry, cloves, ginger and cinnamon. Mr Posnett knew how to sing 'The Lost Chord' at the piano, and did it so well that it had never occurred to him to learn to play anything else, not even the plantation songs of Stephen Foster.

In those days, if you stood before the fire on a cold night, your front became very hot if you were facing it, and your back became very cold. Then you would turn round and shiver as your front cooled down and your back warmed up. Old ladies who knitted or read by the fireside would develop one mottled leg unless they changed from one side of the fire to the other often enough.

The greatest fire was the one in the marketplace. This was a tradition in that town, whose origin was completely unknown. There had always been a Christmas fire as well as a Guy Fawkes one, and that was that. There would be a man selling hot sausages and pies, a woman selling beer, and somebody else making cocoa.

Just before Jim's first Christmas, Alfie said, 'I want it to snow! I want it to snow!'

'Oh, don't,' said Mr Ginger Leghorn. 'It messes up the trains like nobody's business, and there's all that shovelling to do, and putting salt on the platform, and then the snow gets too heavy on top of the signals, and it gets in the works and freezes up, and the points get frozen solid, and three miles down the line a whopping great branch falls off a tree. And there's always some poor old codger who goes arse … who keels over and breaks his hip. Don't wish for snow, Alfie, my lad. We might get some.'

'But we can make a snowman, and whizz down the hill on the tea tray! And have snowball fights.'

'Two snowmen side by side,' said Mr Ginger Leghorn, striking his joke-telling pose. 'Guess what the first one said to the other one. He said … "I can smell carrots!"'

'Oh, Dad!' chorused the children.

'I'm going to do my snow dance,' said Alfie.

'A snow dance; this is something I've got to see,' said his father. 'Let's be having it, then.'

Alfie began to jump from side to side, raising an arm and a leg together as he hopped from one foot to another. 'Let it snow!' he chanted.

'Let it snow!
Let it snow!
Let it snow!
So that we don't have to go
To go to go to go to school
Tomorrow!'

'That looks tiring,' said Ginger. 'Where'd you get that from? Did you make it up?'

'He got it from Sophie at school,' said Sissy.

'And Sophie got it from Caroline,' said Beryl.

'Well, it's a rum little dance,' said Mr Ginger Leghorn. 'But there isn't any school tomorrow anyway. Let's just hope it doesn't work.'

But it did. It worked exactly the right amount. The chill intensified, and a light snow began to fall gently during the night, the delicate flakes dancing about in the small breaths of wind, until by morning three inches had settled on the roofs and pavements. Out in the backyard Tildo tentatively placed one paw in front of the other as he tried out the unfamiliar, crunchy new carpet, and Jim stood with his forepaws on the windowsill, whining with excited incomprehension.

Mr Ginger Leghorn looked out and was satisfied that his beloved GWR would not be having too much bother, and the children ran straight outside with woolly hats and mittens on, to make snowballs and thrust them down each other's necks. 'There'll soon be tears,' said Mr Ginger Leghorn, and 'Wonder who'll get hurt first,' said Molly.

It was Beryl, who slipped and cracked her knee on the cobbles, but she soon recovered, and returned to the fray. Then Sissy cried because Alfie put too much snow down the back of her collar. Then Albert slipped and broke a tooth against the railings, but luckily it was only a milk tooth, and was due for replacement anyway, and the split lip would repair itself soon enough.

The following evening the town's brass band, who had been practising their carols for weeks, and the Salvation Army band too, marched into the town square from different directions, their bass drums booming, playing different tunes in different keys, competing very ably with each other for volume and verve. One or two bandsmen skidded on a patch of ice in their hobnails, bringing about some interesting mayhem, and a few entertainingly elephantine oompahs.

Usually, on this occasion, it would be raining, or too cold and windy, or the fire would not light properly, but this was one year that everybody would always remember. The night was fine and starlit, the air was still, and everybody who ought to be there was there. Mr Draggit brought a brazier and sold piping-hot, slightly charcoaled chestnuts in small brown paper bags. The crisp air was full of the sweet scent of the roasting, and people squealed and blew on their fingers as they peeled their chestnuts open.

The particularly memorable thing was that the Leghorns brought along their family dog, who wore a galvanised bucket on his head and howled melodiously and mournfully along to the strains of 'In the Bleak Midwinter', 'O Come, All Ye Faithful' and 'Silent Night'. Mr Ginger Leghorn told Alfie to take Jim home, but the crowd would have none of it, and in subsequent years people would ask him, 'You bringing the dog to the carols, Ginger?' It was a rare and wondrous thing, a dog with a bucket on his head who could sing more or less in key, and every year it made the papers.

There was more snow on the following day, and the children wrapped themselves in scarves and coats and mittens, and went up the hill behind the railway cottages with tin trays. Their breath turned to steam in the freezing air, and their faces turned red. Alfie threw snowballs for Jim to catch, until his snout and head were covered with a fine dusting of snow. With Jim running behind them, they hurtled down, crashed into the fence, and trudged back up again until they were completely exhausted and their hands were blue with cold, so that, once back in the warmth of the house, they ached and stung as soon as they began to thaw out. In the house there were big baked potatoes waiting to be put in their pockets so that they could go back out again. Jim began to limp, and it turned out that snow had clagged up the fur between his pads. Mr Ginger Leghorn rolled the dog on his back, and sorted out the problem while Jim wriggled about and attempted to bite his hands.

On Christmas morning the children awoke to find that they each had a stocking at the foot of their beds, filled with pencils, boiled sweets, Acme whistles, felt glove puppets and enormous oranges. Alfie swore that during the night he had woken up to see Father Christmas attaching his to the end of the bed. Later that day Tildo and Jim went bonkers among the wrapping paper, and knocked things over so that the family had to panic as they dealt with all the fallen candles. Tildo was given a catnip mouse and a ping-pong ball to play with, and Jim received an enormous postman's leg. He liked his bones rotten and stinky, so he spent half an hour burying it in a flower bed, so that he could dig it up again in the new year. Then he spent the next couple of weeks gnawing away at its delightful disgustingness until it no longer tasted of anything at all, and finally he reburied it, just in case. For the rest of the year, Jim mostly had to make do with modest presents of paddywack, beef ribs and mutton bones.

On Christmas evening, Mr Ginger Leghorn decided to roast some chestnuts on the glowing coals of the fire, and he arranged them in a neat pattern on the long-handled roasting pan. He forgot to pierce the nuts first, however, and they all exploded at pretty much the same moment, sending Tildo straight up the curtains from the surprise of it, and Station Jim under the table. Ginger got a very hot fragment down his shirt collar, which made him dance and hop and swear awhile as he tried to extract it, and Mrs Molly Leghorn spilled some cream onto the table from the shock of it. The children said, 'Cor, Dad, put some more on and do it again!' and Sissy deposited Tildo in front of the little white lake so he could clean up the spillage.

STATION CAT

At Jim's station there was a cat that he mostly succeeded in avoiding, because it was really a signal-box cat. The signal box was some way down the track, and it contained two signalmen, called Mr Sharpe and Mr Simnick. Their real names were an irrelevance, however, because they were known by their nicknames. Mr Sharpe was known as 'Curly' because he was completely bald, and Mr Simnick was known as 'Titch', because he was absolutely enormous. His hands were the size of plates, and finding the right size in shoes was a nightmare. People liked to say that he could have hired out his shoes for rowing boats, and others said he was the human version of Bonaparte, the mastiff at the coaching inn.

Titch and Curly worked upstairs in the signal box, where they had a bank of beautiful brass levers with which to adjust the points in the tracks. They handled the levers with oily rags in their hands because they didn't want the sweat of their hands to tarnish the sparkling brass, and both of them were very brawny in the shoulders because of the physical effort of operating their elaborate system of levers and greased cables.

It was a highly responsible job, and Titch and Curly were proud that there had never been an accident on their patch because of the levers being adjusted wrongly. Their lanterns were always primed with lamp oil, and their flags were always immaculate. They even had a sewing kit to mend any tears or sew on patches, and a pot of varnish to smarten up the flagsticks.

Inside their signal box there was a little coal fire for the cold days, and for that all they had to do was fetch coal that fell from the huge hopper that replenished the tenders. The only manner in which they were ever dishonest was in sneaking lumps of coal home after work, for their own fires and ranges. It was what they called 'their little perk'. In those days the houses were cold and draughty, people had little money, and being warm in winter was the nicest thing in the world.

Their stove in the signal box had a circular metal plate on top for boiling a kettle, and both men were always so full of thick, milky, sugary tea that they had to pop downstairs and out into the bushes every ten minutes. Curly smoked Capstan Full Strength, and Titch smoked Woodbines. Like everyone else in those days they had the bad luck of not knowing that smoking is a deadly habit; you could even buy a brand with cork tips that was advertised as being good for your lungs.

Titch and Curly, snug in their signal box in a fug of smoke, mainly talked about the old days when they were young and used to go poaching together, and also about the royal family, who were always reported as doing or about to do something in the daily press. From the way they talked, you'd think they knew the royals personally, which, in a way, they did, because King Edward and Queen Alexandra occasionally passed through in the Royal Train, and once the King had surprised them in their signal box when his train was taking on water and he had fancied a stroll. At the moment he turned up, Titch was coming back from the bushes, doing up his flies, and he had the horrible thought that he might have to shake the King's hand without having washed it first. He and Curly had been so tongue-tied that they could think of nothing to do but pat the King's dog on the head, and bow repeatedly, until the King told them to stop and asked them to tell him about their families. When he left, the King's dog, Caesar, weed on the bottom of the steps, and to make up for it His Majesty gave Curly and Titch an enormous cigar each, which they treasured too much to smoke, and which are still preserved by their descendants more than a hundred years later.

Several times a day they would amble down the track to inspect the points, and with them ambled Mr Jenkinson, the station cat, known as 'Jenks' for short.

Jenks was a sociable silver tabby cat who took an interest in the milk that went into the signalmen's tea, and spent much of his ample spare time foraging on the embankments for mice and voles, and the occasional rabbit. His greatest conquest had been a cock pheasant, which Curly had taken home for his family when Jenks had declined to eat it.

When a train came in Jenks would hurry along and sit next to the stationmaster, who was checking tickets at the platform exit. This was an excellent place to receive pats on the head, ear fondling and chucks under the chin. Best of all, it was the ideal place to collect the titbits that regular passengers saved for him from their sandwiches. Oddly enough, his second favourite thing was Gentleman's Relish, which most people think is absolutely vile. It tastes of rotten anchovies, but, inexplicably, some people love it. Because he received so many morsels from passing passengers, Curly and Titch never had to feed him themselves.

His very favourite thing was haddock, lightly poached in milk. It was brought to him every day by Lady Huffington, known locally as 'Huffanpuff' because she was somewhat large and unwieldy, with a great big red face under the most enormous floral hats.

On the surface, Lady Huffanpuff was a jolly and friendly person who was kind and generous with everyone. She had a powerful voice and an enormous laugh, spreading merriment wherever she appeared. She lived in a vast empty house on the hillside above the town, and had almost no money at all. Her sons had gone away and died in South Africa in the Boer War, her daughter had married and gone to America, and her husband had disappeared to Singapore, whence he occasionally sent cheques for very small sums. Lady Huffanpuff earned a tiny income for herself by translating French novels into English for a publisher in London, and so she liked to sprinkle her speech with French expressions.

Lady Huffanpuff turned up with poached haddock every day, and dined off it herself in the evenings, along with a mug of sherry and piles of heavily buttered bread.

She felt that she and Jenks were kindred spirits. When she went to the station with his haddock, he wound himself round her stumpy legs and purred.

One morning Curly and Titch came in to work early and found that Jenks was not in his basket, where he would normally have been asleep on one of Curly's old jumpers. 'Out mousing,' they thought. But he was not there the next day, nor the day after, and then they began to worry. They walked for miles down the track to see if he had been run over by a train, and found not a trace. They called his name, and looked under things and inside things, and on top of things. They put up a notice in the station, which read:

MISSING.
MR JENKINSON (JENKS)
HAVE YOU SEEN OUR TABY CAT?
YELER EYES, WHITE SOCKS, WONKY BLACK
MOUSETACH, VERY TALKERTIVE.
ALL INFUMATION GREATEFLY RECEIVED.
APLY TO TICKET OFFICE.

After a week, Curly and Titch were down in the dumps, but becoming reconciled to the thought that they had lost

Jenks forever, until one evening somebody came up the steps of the signal box, and tapped on the door.

It was Ginger, accompanied by Station Jim.

'Still looking for Jenks?' enquired Ginger, and Curly and Titch nodded sadly.

'No sign of him,' said Titch.

'Not a dicky bird,' confirmed Curly.

'Well, I've had an idea,' said Ginger. 'I'm doing the yeomanry this weekend, and I'll be seeing an acker of mine.'

Accordingly, on Monday evening Smiffy turned up at the signal box with Sniffy, Jim, Mr Ginger Leghorn and the children, all in a posse of eagerness.

Curly and Titch looked sceptically at the lugubrious bloodhound, who was, like his master, covered with soot and coal dust from the forge. 'You reckon he can do it, then?' asked Curly.

'Just give him something to sniff,' said Smiffy. 'It's almost guaranteed.'

Titch went and got the old jumper from Jenks's bed and held it out to the dog. 'Here, sniff that,' he said.

Sniffy didn't need to be told 'Go seek'. Bloodhounds are inclined to become instantly obsessed by any new smell, and can follow one for a hundred miles, given a chance. When following a smell, they refuse to obey any commands, and all you can do is let them drag you along. Sniffy had a special harness with a strong leather lead on it, so that he could pull Smiffy in his wake without choking.

Without hesitation, Sniffy sniffed the jumper, put his nose to the ground, and wandered in circles around the small cabin. Then he went down the steps, sniffed in a few more circles, threw his head back and belled, and set off through the woods on the north side of the track. Jim wanted to play, but Sniffy ignored him completely, now that he had more important things to do. Up they went, following a path so narrow that it was really only good for children and foxes. Ginger noticed that quite a few twigs had been snapped, so something large must have passed that way.

Sniffy belled again, throwing his head up and singing with the pleasure of the hunt.

By the time that they arrived at Lady Huffington's house they were scratched up, dirty and exhausted, apart from Sniffy, who sat and sang, watched from the window with great horror by Jenks, who bared his teeth and hissed through the glass. Curly pulled on the big brass lever in the porch, and a bell rang inside the house.

When Lady Huffington came to the door and opened it, Sniffy tried to pull Smiffy indoors to get to the cat, but Smiffy managed to haul him back and restrain him. Lady Huffington went pale when she saw Curly and Titch, but said, 'Yes? Can I help you?'

'I'm sorry, My Lady,' said Curly, 'but we've come for the cat. You've got to give him back.'

'You can't just go nicking people's cats,' added Titch, 'it ain't right.'

'What cat?' asked Lady Huffington.

'Our cat Jenks,' said Titch. 'That one in the window that's hissing at Sniffy.'

Lady Huffington turned and saw Jenks, and said, 'But … but … but …'

'No buts, My Lady. You've got to hand him over.'

To everyone's surprise, Lady Huffington put her back against the pillar of the porch, and began to slide down it, until she was sitting on the ground with her legs splayed out. Her great round red face crumpled up, and big tears began to follow each other down her cheeks. Curly and Titch didn't know what to do, so they just stood there in bewilderment. Jim whined and placed a paw on her shoulder.

Albert and Sissy followed his lead, and they went up to Lady Huffington and gave her a hug, whereupon she began to cry even more. She cried about being lonely in that big shabby house with its neglected garden, she cried about her husband and daughter being abroad, she cried about not being young and beautiful any more, she cried about having nothing to look forward to, and she cried about having been caught out as nothing better than a cat thief. Most of all she cried at the thought of having to give up Jenks. There were a great many tears.

'Please don't cry, Lady Huffanpuff,' said Albert.

'Is that what you call me, *mes enfants*?' sobbed Lady Huffington.

'It's only out of friendliness,' said Ginger Leghorn. 'They don't mean nothing by it.'

'No, we do like you really,' said Sissy.

This made her sob again, and at last Curly had a brainwave. 'I'll go in and put the kettle on.' Some minutes later he came back out with a cup of tea, with two lumps of sugar on the saucer, just in case. Lady

Huffington sipped at it, still seated on the ground at the base of the pillar. Finally she said, 'Would you help me up?' and Titch and Curly extended their hands to heave her upright. 'Thank you so much. You'll find a box in the pantry. You can put Jenks in that, and I can bid him *au revoir.*'

As they all walked away with Jenks yeowling in the box, they felt not in the least bit triumphant. Instead, they were extremely sad. Even Sniffy seemed subdued, now that he had no scent to follow.

'Makes you think, doesn't it?' said Titch.

'Certainly does,' said Curly.

'Poor Lady Huffanpuff,' said the children.

'Shows you can even be a Lady and still not have nothing much,' said Titch.

The story, however, has an unexpectedly happy ending, and not just because Curly and Titch gave Sniffy a huge thank-you bone from the butcher's. Mr Jenkinson had rather liked it at Lady Huffington's, so he took to disappearing from the signal box and going to visit her. He found her in the same way as Sniffy had, as cats also have a very fine sense of smell. It was summer, and Lady Huffington took to leaving a window open for him, but then as autumn drew in, she had a cat flap cut into the kitchen door. Whenever Jenks turned up, she telephoned down to the signal box to let Curly and Titch know where he was.

Happier still, the children took to calling round occasionally after school, sometimes bringing Station Jim with them, and Lady Huffington made small batches of rock cakes and scones, with strawberry jam. She remembered all their birthdays, and bought them Ludo, jigsaw puzzles, dominoes, bagatelle, a shove-ha'penny board, a dog on wheels that played the xylophone, and a pack of cards. She had a swing put up on the walnut tree in the garden, and would sit on the terrace remembering how wonderful it had been when her own children were little. Molly Leghorn used to say, 'We've got the poshest babysitter in England. Blimey, whatever next?' Sometimes she and Ginger went round with the children to have tea with her, and they sat there at the table with its lacy cloth, not quite sure what to say, and wondering why you had to have a special knife for butter, and what to do with their cake forks. They never invited her round to their house, but Lady Huffanpuff quite understood why. They felt that their house was too little and humble for a Lady, and neither were they themselves nearly posh enough.

Lady Huffanpuff's lonely life in her great big house made the children feel grateful to be living in their smoky railway cottage on a terrace, all in a bundle of people and cats and dogs and lazy pigeons, and Ginger liked to say, 'You know what? I bet even the King gets a bit low, sometimes, with his palaces and all. That's why he's got that little dog, to perk him up, probably.'

STATION JIM'S SECOND
FINEST HOUR

Jim loved sausages more than anything else in the world, and didn't care if they were cooked or not. They were the one thing that made him misbehave. He was banned from all the local butchers' shops, and if there were sausages on the table he could leap up and lunge at the same time, or he would suddenly appear on your lap and stick his face in your plate. When they were having bangers and mash or toad-in-the-hole, the Leghorns would put Station Jim out of the back door, leaving him to howl with longing and despair in the yard.

One day Station Jim was sniffing about on the pavement in front of the railway cottages, when he thought he smelled sausages. He raised his nose and whiffled at the breeze. These were pork sausages with quite a lot of fat in them, and about twenty per cent cereal, at some considerable distance, probably down at the docks, because Jim could also smell the green scent of the sea.

Without further thought, because sausages were an absolute priority, Jim set off on his quest. He went down the hill, past the railway station and the post office, the town pump and the horse trough, the town hall and the police station, and when he found himself down at the docks he had no further distance to go than up the gangplank of a collier.

This collier was a medium-sized tubby and rugged ship so engrained with shiny coal dust that even the most violent rains and storms at sea never fully managed to clean it off. The crew were also engrained and shiny with coal dust, and whenever they eventually got home to Newcastle in between voyages, their wives would bring a tin bath to the parlour and fill it with hot water so that they could stand in it and scrub themselves down. When they saw themselves in the mirror, they would be surprised to recognise themselves, and their wives would say, 'Why aye, it is you then,' and their clean husbands would reply, 'Aye, hinny, it's me. Who were you hoping for?' Their children would say, 'Coaly Dad's got back, and now he's Cleaned-Up Dad,' because in their minds they had two completely different fathers all rolled up into one.

Jim went down the steep gangways into the galley, his ears and jowls flopping forwards, and great concentration on his face as he coped with the metal steps. The galley was a tiny little room with a table that had a raised rim around it so that things could not slide off at sea, and all the implements were hung up on hooks. There was a strong scent of sausages there, but the sad thing was that the crew had eaten them all and gone ashore for the last time before setting off back to Newcastle. All that was left were the dirty plates on the table. Jim washed them up with his tongue, and relished the flavours of brown sauce, buttery mashed potatoes, peas covered with gravy, and delicious sausage grease. It wasn't much, but it was worth the long walk. Jim then settled down and fell asleep under the table.

'Blimey,' said Ginger Leghorn two days later, taking off his cap and scratching the top of his head as he stood on the docks and gazed out to sea, 'what the heck's this, then?'

'Well,' said Smiffy, 'if Sniffy says that this is where Jim is, then this is where Jim is.'

'Out at sea?' He turned and looked down at Sniffy. 'Are you sure about this, boy?'

Sniffy looked back up at him, closed his eyes, lifted his head, and belled.

'Jim's gone for a swim? I don't believe it. Not out there. Just look at those waves.'

The whole family were so grief-stricken at the news that Jim had apparently swum away to sea that they sat miserably at teatimes and could hardly eat. At night the children cried, and the cat sat in the yard and yeowled. Molly and Ginger Leghorn kept shaking their heads and repeating, 'I don't believe it. Why would he do a thing like that? Must have had a rush of blood.'

'Lucky he's got a collar on,' said Molly Leghorn. 'When they find his body they can let us know.'

They were just getting used to the idea that Jim had inexplicably committed suicide by swimming out to sea, when someone came from the post office bringing a telegram.

Mrs Leghorn was better at reading than Ginger, so she read it out to him, exclaiming 'Blimey!' and 'Blow me!' at the same time.

GONE TO NEWCASTLE STOP LOVELY TIME STOP LOVELY SAUSAGES NICE BLACK PUDDING STOP BACK AT DOCKS ON TUESDAY 1200 HRS WEATHER PERMITTING STOP JIM

Ginger telephoned the harbourmaster from the station, and found out that the SS *Pride of Blyth* was due in at that time, with a cargo of coal.

The story got around the town very quickly, because it was so extraordinary, and Jim had become such a popular dog. Many people had shaken their heads with sorrow over Jim's suicide, feeling great sympathy for the Leghorns, and now they were all overjoyed and terribly surprised. When the Mayor heard about it, he said to the Deputy Mayor, 'How about a little celebration?'

The Deputy Mayor played trombone in the town band, and in the Salvation Army band too, so that evening he went round town after work, knocking on doors, and the folk he called on went in turn and called on their employers to see if they could have the morning off. Miss Fortunata Horseferry, the schoolteacher, agreed that the children could have the morning off too. The dockers were going to be at the docks anyway, and the *Pride of Blyth* was the only ship due in. The Mayor was going to come with his chain of office about his neck, and the town crier was dispatched about the streets with his black tricorn hat, his red frock coat and his big brass bell, to cry 'Oyez! Oyez!' and summon the populace for Tuesday at noon.

The plan worked better than expected because the ship docked half an hour early, and the Mayor was able to go on board and tell the crew what was going to happen.

And that is why Station Jim had a civic reception down on the docks, with children cheering as he was led down the gangplank to the blare of the combined bands playing 'A Life on the Ocean Wave' and 'What Shall We Do With the Drunken Sailor?'. When Station Jim realised that his family were all there waiting to meet him, he threw himself about in such a frenzy of joy that he slipped the leash, leaping and capering so much that Ginger and the children had to defend their faces with their arms or they would have been licked to death. At the same time he managed to sing a dogsong, consisting of whines and howls and small yips. In the newspaper the next day there was a photograph of Station Jim, apparently flying, with his lips drawn up in such a grin that his whole face seemed to consist of nothing but pink gums and shiny white teeth.

When Station Jim finally calmed down, the Mayor made a long speech full of classical references to dogs that he had found in an encyclopaedia. Lady Huffanpuff, dressed in a highly floral style, made a shorter one, and presented Station Jim with a certificate of welcome and a new disc for his collar with 'Home is the Sailor' engraved on the back of it. Everybody posed for a picture to be printed in the *Herald and Advertiser*, and there was a separate picture of Smiffy and Sniffy.

Ginger Leghorn took the collier's crew to the Tipsy Boatswain to buy them a pint each, and heard the story of how they had found the dog under the galley table half an hour after setting off, how it had made itself at home and stolen sausages from the cupboard. They told him that Jim had spent the days up on deck, barking at the seagulls and trying to bite the spray that came up over the guardrails.

Molly and the children took Jim upriver and threw sticks for him so that he could swim out and wash off some of the coal dust. Then they brought him home and washed him again, out in the yard. Tildo waited till he was dry, and then wound himself in and out of Jim's legs, bumping his head and purring. Mrs Leghorn told everyone to change their clothes, because Jim had covered them all in coal dust, and she mashed them in the cauldron with a wooden dolly to get them clean.

The story of Station Jim's voyage and civic reception made it into the national press, and for a few weeks he even received fan mail. In France one of the national newspapers printed the story in order to demonstrate how mad the British are. A local photographer printed a large photograph of the Leghorn family with Station Jim sitting in front of them with his favourite galvanised bucket on his head. This and the newspaper articles were pinned up at the station for the passengers to look at, and at the town hall too. At Windsor Castle, King Edward read them and showed them to the Queen, saying, 'Plucky little fellow, eh?' and he turned to his own small dog, Caesar, and said, 'Don't you go trying anything like that.'

The person who was most pleased about Station Jim's return was Smiffy. Even he had had his doubts about whether Jim had really gone out to sea, but now he had been vindicated, or, rather, his bloodhound had. Back in his forge, he patted Sniffy on the head, saying 'Who's a good boy, then?', and all his pride in his dog's infallibility came flooding back.

SCHOOL

On days when the trains were not running because of works on the line, Jim went to school with the children.

It was a small Church of England National school which consisted of one large room. There was a raised dais at the front, with a desk on it for the teacher, and behind it on the wall, a very large blackboard. There were several rows of desks for the children, with the bench seats built in. It was considered a matter of personal honour to carve your name in your desk without being detected.

They had lids that opened up, and each child stored their slates, books and pencils inside. Above the hinge, on the right-hand side, there was an inkwell for the children to use for their dip pens, which were regularly topped up with a horrible greeny-black ink that seemed to get everywhere: on your hands, on your face, on your clothes, and very occasionally onto your sheets of paper. The ink didn't come off even if you scrubbed yourself raw with a pumice stone when you reached home.

Upon one wall was a large portrait print of His and Her Majesties, looking most royal and gracious in their colourful regalia, and on another was a print of a pale Jesus, dressed in white robes, with a splendid golden halo about his head, and a sheep slung across his shoulders. Underneath it said, in elaborate lettering, 'The Good Shepherd'.

At the back was a large wooden board with the Ten Commandments written on it in Gothic script, some of which were never explained to the children, so that generations would grow up thinking that it was sinful to become an adult, and wondering why you would want to cover your neighbour's ox or his ass or his wife.

The teacher at this school was a terrifying, raspy-voiced, tennis-playing lady named Miss Fortunata Horseferry, but the children knew her by many other names, such as 'Whacker'. She was a tall, slender woman in middle age, with her grey hair piled up on her head. She wore a white apron to protect her dresses from the grubbiness of children, and she wore pince-nez glasses, over which she could peer disapprovingly, should anyone become unduly cheerful or boisterous. She had been a teacher for twenty-five years, and her head was full of lessons which she could use over and over again as one generation succeeded another.

In her hand she always held a yardstick, marked out in feet and inches, but seldom used for measuring. It was employed for pointing to things she had written on the blackboard, and for whacking badly behaved children on the top of the head. If they were very bad, she would make them put out their hands, palm downwards, and strike them across the knuckles with the narrow edge. This was excruciatingly painful. If a child was particularly stupid or ignorant, they would be made to stand in the corner wearing a tall dunce's cap with a big D on it.

Under Miss Horseferry's tutelage, Alfie, Arthur, Beryl, Sissy and Albert learned the lengths in yards of miles, rods, poles and perches, the number of ounces in a pound and of pounds in stones and of stones in hundredweights and tons. They recited the times tables both backwards and forwards, and learned by heart poems by William Wordsworth and Henry Newbolt. They were required to remember the dates of every English monarch, going back to King Ethelred the Unready, and every year they would, at least once, be made to trace a large map of the world and shade the dominions of the British Empire in pink, just to make it quite clear that it was indeed an empire upon which the sun never sets.

The children learned about tea growing in Ceylon, rubber production in the Amazon, the parables and miracles of Jesus Christ, the victories of the English over the French in the Hundred Years War, and about how King Edward the Fourth drowned his brother in a butt of malmsey wine, without their ever learning what a butt was.

To the accompaniment of Miss Horseferry caterwauling, clattering and jangling on the upright piano, they sang hymns, such as 'We Plough the Fields and Scatter' and 'There is a Green Hill Far Away, Without a City Wall', only to wonder for the rest of their lives why you would all run away after ploughing, and why a green hill might have a city wall round it in the first place. Every day they recited the Lord's Prayer, and it was not until she was twelve that Beryl realised that God's name was not Harold.

The children quite liked their school, because in those days nobody expected their teachers to be kind or gentle, or even remotely reasonable.

And Miss Fortunata 'Whacker' Horseferry did have a big weak spot, which was that she loved animals. Children who tried to bring their cats in always failed, because cats don't go to school, on the grounds that they know everything worth knowing already, but others might come in with a mouse in their pocket, or a tortoise, or a scrabbly brainless rabbit, and, without fail, Miss Horseferry would go damp-eyed and soppy. She particularly liked it when Jim came in with the Leghorn children, because Jim would bound up to her and try to cover her with wet kisses, making her feel lovable after all.

In later life, the children's memory of their schooldays would be not of Miss Horseferry as a terrible dragon, but as the tall, slender lady who used to take the whole class up the hillside above the town, ostensibly to teach them about clouds, wild flowers and the wonders of nature, but really to throw a tennis ball for the dog.

RAGGABONE

In those days there were many tradesmen who patrolled the streets, hawking their wares, and each had a special cry.

There was the muffin man, for example, and the tins man who put new linings in your copper pots, and the scissor man who had a water wheel for sharpening your scissors and knives, and the tinker, who could mend your pots and pans, and the cat's-meat man who brought horsemeat from the knackers' yard.

> Cat's meat! Cat's meat!
> Make your cats fat meat!
> The dog might like some too … ooo.

There were diddicoys, who knew how to mend machinery, there was the pieman, who pushed a handcart loaded with hand-raised pork pies, and steak-and-kidney pies, and Cornish pasties, and beef-and-potato pies, and any other kind of pie he felt like making on the day. He used to chant

Simple Simon met a pieman
Going to the fair
Said Simple Simon to the pieman
'What have you got there?'
Said the pieman to Simple Simon
'Pies, you idiot.'

He chanted the word 'idiot' as if it were the amen from the end of a psalm.

There was a man with a scrapyard who collected anything metal that was broken or unwanted. He had a cart, and a piebald cob with blinkers at its eyes and its face always in a haybag, and he would go up and down every street once a week calling out 'Any old iron! Any old iron!' Back at the yard he would sort the metal into its different kinds, and take it out to the big forge, or to Smiffy's smaller one, where it would be turned back into useful things.

The Any Old Iron Man lived at his yard, with his horse and a three-legged mongrel called Tripod. He had a big lean-to against the back of the station wall, with a coal-burning stove that he fuelled with coal that spilled from the trains when they were refuelling. Mr Leghorn and the other railwaymen pretended not to notice, because it saved anyone from having to clear up the spillage, and they weren't entirely innocent themselves. A railwayman's cottage was always warm.

The Any Old Iron Man cooked for himself and the dog on top of the stove, and what he ate was a constantly evolving stew. Every day he would put something new in to make up for what he had eaten the day before, and this could be anything from a carrot to a marrowbone. It would be heated up and eaten with dunked bread, and every day it was the same but a little bit different. As he became older and his teeth began to fall out, he would simply put in things that were less chewy, until, by the time he reached eighty, it was more of a soup than a stew. After his meal he would sleep soundly on a heap of sacking, warmed up by Tripod and the lingering heat of the stove.

There was another man, the poorest of the lot, who also had a cart, and a pony with blinkers and a haybag. Most men of his kind only had a handcart, so Mr Spirtle counted himself lucky, even though he never earned more than sixpence a day. He was the Rag-and-Bone Man. He was bald on top, with lanky grey hair at the sides and back. He had a crooked spine, was very thin, and he dressed in the best and cleanest of the rags that he collected. Sometimes he was obliged to wind rags about his feet when no one had recently discarded any shoes. All day, every day, he would trundle slowly through the streets calling 'Raggabone! Raggabone! Raggabone!' and people would bring him out any useful rubbish they might have. Mr Spirtle received threepence a pound for white rag, and tuppence a pound for coloured. For bones he also raised tuppence a pound. The rags went for making paper, and the bones could be made into knife handles, ornaments and little toys. Sometimes he sold them to people who made chemicals, and any fat left on them could be scraped off and sold for making soap.

Some people called him a totter, and others a bone-grubber, but Mr Spirtle called himself a Rag-and-Bone Man. His was the most humble job on earth, but he had some pride. If anyone gave him anything particularly useful, he would give them a donkey stone, so that it would be fair swaps, and not just taking. These donkey stones were used for cleaning up doorsteps and making them non-slip, and there were whole streets full of women who spent hours every week on their knees, making sure that theirs was the best and non-slippiest of all. That time down on your knees, scrubbing alongside your neighbours doing the same, was the explanation for the lightning spread of gossip back in the old days.

One day Mr Spirtle passed Number 4 Railway Cottages, just as Station Jim was sitting outside, waiting for any dogs to pass by that might be worth sniffing. It was in the evening, after a long day, and Mr Spirtle was tired and hungry, with very little to look forward to. His pony was tired too, and they were going slowly. It was impossible not to notice that between his feet, Station Jim had a big knuckle bone that must have weighed at least a pound. That bone was worth a whole tuppence.

Mr Spirtle stopped the cart, and called out 'Raggabone! Raggabone! Raggabone!', as if this would stir Station Jim's conscience, and induce him to take pity on the poor old man. It failed to work. Instead, Jim sniffed at the air and detected a large number of bones on the back of Mr Spirtle's cart. Abandoning his own bone, he trotted out into the street, and hopped up into the back of the cart, where he began to ferret about in the rags.

'Here, you! Get off!' cried Mr Spirtle. 'Get off, yer little bleeder!'

But Jim would not get off. He carried on burrowing away with his forelegs, letting out little barks of anticipation.

'Right,' said Mr Spirtle. 'If you're after my bones, I'm having yours!' and he went to the doorstep and picked up Jim's knuckle bone.

As he straightened up, he came face-to-face with Mrs Leghorn, who had come to the door to see what all the shouting and yipping was about.

'What are you doing, nicking my dog's bone?' she said, putting her hands on her hips, and scowling down at him.

He gestured towards the dog on the back of the cart, and said, 'Well, he's nicking mine, isn't he?'

Mrs Leghorn looked up, and called out, 'Jim! Jim! Get off that cart, and get in at once!'

In the end she had to drag him off by the collar and shove him indoors. 'Sorry about that,' she said.

'Dogs will be dogs,' said Mr Spirtle.

Mrs Leghorn looked up and down the length of Mr Spirtle. He was a sorry sight indeed. His shoes were not a pair, and the left one had the sole flapping off it. His trousers were too short, were held up by a cord through the belt loops, knotted in a bow at the front, and were split across the knees. He wore a cardigan with most of the buttons missing, but no shirt beneath it, and his jacket had the filthiest cuffs she had ever seen. Around his neck he had knotted a brown tie, despite having no collar around which to tie it. Mrs Leghorn shuddered inside at the thought of having to work so hard only in order to live in such terrible poverty. She looked into his tired old eyes, and thought, 'He's human too. I'm just a lot luckier.'

'I've got heaps of bones in the garden,' she said. 'When Jim's chewed all the life out of them, he leaves them in a corner. Do you want 'em?'

'Heaps?'

'Well, a heap.'

'I'd like that very much, missus,' said Mr Spirtle.

It turned out to be a whole sackful. Then Mrs Leghorn said, 'If you go up behind the house on the hillside, there's a dead sheep there. It's been there for months. Should be easy to clear it all up. The ravens've picked it clean.'

'I'm very grateful to you, missus.'

'And while you're up there I'll make you some bread and dripping, and a mug of cocoa.'

'Bread and dripping, missus? I'm much obliged.'

It was a good day all round; Mrs Leghorn got rid of Jim's bone collection, Jim found a pleasantly disgusting mutton bone on the cart, and Mr Spirtle had his first slice of bread and dripping in days. He arrived back to his hovel just as the gaslighter was beginning his rounds, and put out a bucket of oats for his pony. Tomorrow he would sort through his rags and bones, and see what the day would bring.

Tomorrow he would not have to crawl through the streets on his hands and knees, looking for horseshoe nails between the cobbles, and he would drop off three donkey stones for Mrs Leghorn, because fair exchange is no robbery, and that sheep's skull would be worth tuppence all on its own.

STATION JIM'S FINEST HOUR

His Majesty King Edward was by now much too fat, quite old, and very unhealthy. He smoked a great many cigars, because he had no idea they were bad for him, and was so out of breath that when he went to play golf someone had to carry a chair for him to recover in after he'd played each shot. He knew that he was not going to live very much longer, had become tired and sad, and was only prevented from abdicating by his friends.

It seemed likely that his German cousin was working himself up to start a war quite soon, the people of Ireland were demanding Home Rule, and the two Houses of Parliament were building up to a huge confrontation. The politicians were ignoring his advice. It was not a good time to be King, and he had become one of the few members of the upper classes who was definitely not enjoying the Edwardian age.

Being a king is not as much fun as people imagine it to be, but it has its consolations. One of King Edward's consolations was that he had his own special Royal Train for getting around the country quickly. It was a beautiful train, with all its brass work sparkling, and inside it was very elegant and comfortable indeed. Even this was not as much use as one might have hoped, because in different parts of the country the railway tracks were laid at different distances apart, so that sometimes you had to have two sets of tracks running side by side. When the King used the train, local people would come out in their best clothes to the stations through which he passed, in order to wave and cheer.

It so happened that one day the King and Queen were in the Royal Train, on their way to the West Country, when it had to stop and take on coal and water. The King looked out of his window at the waving and smiling people, and thought it was a little awkward to have them all standing there while nothing very much happened. There had been no arrangement for him to dismount here, but he did not wish to appear rude, so, breathlessly, he struggled to his feet with the help of his cane, and went to the door. He let himself out, handed Queen Alexandra down, and turned and doffed his top hat to the locals who had gathered to cheer him. Everyone cheered even more, and then a little girl ran forward, curtsied awkwardly, and presented

Queen Alexandra with a large Michaelmas daisy she had plucked from the embankment. It was Sissy Leghorn.

Her Majesty patted Sissy on the head, and bent down to say thank you, and at that moment the King spotted Station Jim, with his collecting box about his neck, being held firmly by Ginger Leghorn. Otherwise Station Jim would probably have jumped all over his monarch, who suddenly thought that he'd seen the dog before. This small dog with its enormous toothy grin looked very familiar indeed. The King approached Ginger, who was so over-whelmed that he hardly knew what to do, and asked, 'Is this the dog who went to sea, by any chance?'

'Yes it is, Your Majesty,' replied Ginger, 'if it please Your Majesty.'

'It does please me,' said the King. 'I was very enter-tained when I read about it in the paper. Would you be so kind as to follow me into the train for a minute or two? There's someone I'd like you to meet.'

A tall, distinguished gentleman in an immaculately brushed frock coat and top hat, who had been walking slightly behind the King, leaned forward and said, 'Your Majesty, is this wise?' and the King replied, 'At my time of life, Ponsonby, it's too late for wisdom.'

So it was that Station Jim was formally introduced to Caesar, the King's small black terrier. They sniffed each other cautiously, and gauged each other's mood. Caesar yipped, set his tail into rapid motion, gave a little leap forward, and began a rumbustious play fight that only ended when Ginger and Ponsonby managed to grab them by the collar and pull them apart. 'I'm very sorry, Your Majesty,' said Ginger.

'Nothing to be sorry about, my good man,' replied the King. 'Who'd want a dog that lacks high spirits?'

'Your dog is really very charming,' said the Queen, tickling the end of Jim's nose with the Michaelmas daisy that Sissy had given her. 'I don't think I've seen one quite like him before. What breed is he?'

'Purebred accidental mongrel, ma'am. He's an allsorts,' replied Ginger, and the Queen laughed.

The King bent down to read the legend on Station Jim's collection box. '"Railway Widows and Orphans Fund",' he read, adding a mysterious 'Hmm'. Then he snapped his fingers and said, 'Ponsonby, the purse please.'

'Sit!' said the King, and Station Jim sat, wagging his tail and looking up expectantly, with his head cocked on one side.

'Present arms!' said His Majesty, holding out his right hand, and Station Jim shifted his weight to the left side and presented his paw.

And that is how Station Jim, who had never collected a coin bigger than the half-crown that Mr Hamilton McCosh had given him at the beginning of his career, collected a gold sovereign from the sovereign himself, and met Caesar, who, a few months later was to become famous all over the world when he was photographed following his master's cortège to the funeral at Westminster Abbey.

For the rest of his life, Ginger wished that there had been someone there to take a picture of His Majesty putting a sovereign into Station Jim's box, and then solemnly shaking his paw all over again. Instead, it had to remain as a kind of photograph in his memory, and the story was passed down through his children and his children's children.

They generally conclude the tale with 'Station Jim was quite old by then, and Ginger didn't think that anything better would ever happen to him, so he decided to let him retire and spend the rest of his days as an ordinary family dog'.

So Station Jim retired, and spent his last years grinning, biting chairs, wearing a galvanised iron bucket on his head, chewing bones with his blunted teeth, or fast asleep with Tildo perched upon him like a tea cosy, just an ordinary family dog.

When, after a long and happy life, Jim finally died, the local people quickly raised enough money to have him taken to Mr Packitt, the taxidermist. This gentleman, whose workshop smelled pleasantly of formaldehyde and varnish, mounted him in a sealed glass cabinet, wearing his Railway Widows and Orphans Fund collection box. The case was set up in the entrance of the railway station, with another collection box in the base, and there Station Jim still collects money for charity, more than a hundred years later.

He has one paw raised and a huge grin on his face, and next to him is a small galvanised bucket and a plaster cast of a string of sausages, with the paint fading and flaking off.